BEWITCHMENTS &
BOOKWORMS

A LIBRARY WITCH MYSTERY

ELLE ADAMS

"Not another one!" Aunt Adelaide tipped the book-wyrm off the pages of a large textbook and into the wastepaper basket.

Sylvester the owl came swooping down, stuck his beak into the basket, and grabbed the wriggling book-wyrm before swallowing it whole.

"Ugh," I said. "I didn't need to see that, Sylvester."

He belched loudly. "You're welcome."

Shaking my head, I turned to my aunt. "Where are they all coming from? There isn't another nest… is there?"

We'd barely got rid of the last infestation of paper-eating nuisances that had attempted to gnaw their way through the reference section. This one, however, had come from the box of returned books. Bracing myself, I went to check.

"It's empty, don't worry," Aunt Adelaide said over my shoulder as I peered into the box. "Estelle took the last of the returns upstairs, but if there's a nest, we'll have to deal with it when she's back. One of us should watch the desk, and Cass is… well, I don't know what she has up on the third floor, but it's making a racket."

"Great." Cass had probably brought in another magical monster of some sort. "And Aunt Candace?"

"In her room, no doubt with a magical soundproofing spell on the door. She's working on a new project."

Typical. If nothing else, my family managed to keep life interesting. "I can watch the desk while I repair the book," I offered. "Though I don't know that spell yet…"

"What use is that?" Sylvester remarked. "Did you plan to use superglue instead?"

"That's enough, Sylvester," said Aunt Adelaide. "Sorry. I ought to have already taught you that spell, Rory."

"I've been lucky not to need it." Generally, people had more sense than to damage the property of my family's magical library, but page-eating parasites were an obvious exception. I pulled out the notebook and pen I kept in my pocket. "I can add the word to my Biblio-Witch Inventory afterwards."

Aunt Adelaide nodded and flipped the textbook open, revealing the page the wyrm had chewed through. "Write the word *repair* and picture the page as whole in your mind's eye."

Sylvester closed his eyes and began snoring loudly. I hadn't a clue whether he was genuinely asleep or just being as disrespectful as usual, so I ignored him as I opened a fresh page in my notepad. Then I leaned on the desk to press the point of the pen to the paper. A tingling sensation rushed to my fingertips, and as I wrote the word *repair* on the page, the open textbook in Aunt Adelaide's hands began to shimmer. Ripples passed across the page, and when they faded, the paper was smooth, as if it had never been damaged.

"There we go." Aunt Adelaide beamed, holding the book up to inspect it. "Good as new."

"I'll write the word in my Inventory." I pulled out the thicker book I kept in my pocket, which contained each word—or spell—I'd learned. Once I'd written a word down, all I had to do was tap that word with my fingertip to access its power any time I wanted. Handy, and one of the major perks of being a Biblio-Witch. My family was unique in the magical world, at least according to my Aunt Adelaide, and I'd seen no reason to doubt her.

"I'll return this to where it belongs." Aunt Adelaide closed the textbook. "Can you watch the desk until then?"

"Of course." While she carried the textbook to one of the staircases leading to the upper floors, Jet, my familiar, fluttered over to land beside me on the desk. "Hey, Jet. I thought you were with Aunt Candace."

"She won't let me into her room, partner!" he chirped.

"Weird." Aunt Candace must have been really into her new manuscript if she'd even shut out my familiar. Jet's liking for flying around and listening for gossip had caused my aunt to recruit him as her partner in crime, as she was keen to find new ideas to incorporate into her books. While I didn't necessarily *like* the idea of her monopolising my familiar and using him to spy on people, he seemed happy enough with the arrangement, and he was such a chatterbox that I couldn't work with him hovering over my shoulder all the time.

"Hardly," Sylvester said without opening his eyes. "She gets like this sometimes. You weren't here when she was working on her ten-volume fantasy epic."

"I didn't even know about that one." My aunt had a pen name for every day of the week, and the rest of us weren't allowed into her room when she was immersed in the process—nor were our familiars.

Sylvester was supposedly a familiar, too, though he stretched the definition a little. As the embodiment of the library itself known as a Genius Loci, he'd taken on the form of an owl for reasons known only to himself. Possibly because it meant he got to take more naps, though he didn't technically *need* to sleep.

At least I had company while I watched the desk. My family and I generally took it in turns to keep an eye on the doors, since you never knew who might show up at the library. Sometimes, it was a customer. Sometimes, it was my boyfriend, Xavier, the town's Reaper. And at other times, it was less pleasant company, such as Evangeline, head of the vampires. She hadn't dropped by in a while, but she was my point of contact for updates on the situation with the Founders—a group of dangerous vampires who I'd recently ticked off even further by getting several of them arrested. Oh, and setting one of their houses on fire.

Let's just say the vampires and I had a complicated relationship, not least because my best friend had become one of them upon her own induction to the magical world, while my dad's history with the Founders had landed me in hot water on more than one occasion. More recently, I'd received a threatening note from one Mortimer Vale—the Founders' leader, who was supposed to be in solitary confinement in jail—and unfortunately, Evangeline was my only hope for figuring out how he'd managed to send me that letter. Nobody but her—except possibly the Grim Reaper—had the contacts necessary to find out that kind of information.

Luckily, no vampires showed up at the library that morning, and I was able to help each customer find the books they wanted without too much trouble. Estelle eventually came downstairs, covered in what looked like sawdust, when I was directing an overeager student looking to get ahead on his dissertation to the reference section.

Like the rest of us, my cousin had bright-red hair, and she shared her mother's curvy figure and friendly smile, though her expression was somewhat strained at the moment. "Hey, Rory."

"Hey. It's that way," I added to the student, pointing him to the area behind the front desk. "Just keep walking, and you'll find the right section. Estelle, why are you covered in sawdust?"

My cousin walked around the desk. "Someone accidentally wandered into the Unfinished Section."

"The what?"

"Didn't I already tell you about that?" She tipped some sawdust off the sleeve of her cloak into the wastepaper basket. "It's one of *those* doors. The ones we're not supposed to open without checking first. Anyway, some bright spark left it unlocked. I'd guess Aunt Candace."

"By 'unfinished,' what do you mean?" I asked. "Are the books half written, or…?"

"Some of them are." She joined me behind the desk, unintentionally scattering more sawdust on Sylvester's feathers, which prompted him to give a disgruntled snort. "The section comprises books at all stages of the process. There are unbound pages, some without any writing on them—and sometimes, even the paper isn't finished."

I blinked. "You mean, it's still trees?"

"Trees?" Sylvester opened his eyes. "You have trees in the library and didn't tell me?"

"You know everything that's in here, Sylvester," Estelle said. "In fact, you know the library better than all of us do."

"Now, that doesn't mean I can instantly recall every nook and cranny," he said around a yawn. "Having a vast intellect comes at a price."

"My heart bleeds." I rolled my eyes at him. "Trees in the library. And there I thought I'd seen it all."

Estelle gave a rueful smile. "No such thing in here. For better or worse."

That was true enough. The library contained an endless array of surprises, and even my family hadn't found all of them yet. My grandmother, its creator, had neglected to leave a full list of the library's contents upon her unexpected death, and while Aunt Adelaide had stepped smoothly into the role of head librarian, "helped" by Aunt Candace, that didn't mean she knew all its secrets. Amongst other things, the library contained an invisible floor, a vampire in the basement—and, as I'd just found out, a room full of trees.

"Oh yeah—your mum found another book-wyrm," I told Estelle. "It chewed through a book."

"Another one?" Estelle groaned. "Where?"

"Showed up in the returns basket, I think," I said. "I fixed the book, and she went to take it upstairs, but that was a while ago."

"You don't think she needs our help, does she?" Estelle asked. "Which section?"

"Sylvester?" I'd forgotten whereabouts the book had originally come from, since the library had a lot of areas to keep track of, even if you didn't count the doors that randomly appeared and disappeared on their own schedule.

The owl helpfully closed his eyes again instead of answering.

"I'll find her, partner!" Jet squeaked.

"Thanks, Jet." I gave the owl a pointed look. "See? At least one of us is useful."

"Now, I take exception to that," Sylvester said. "I got rid of your book-wyrm for you."

"All you did was eat it and then take a nap." Embodiment of the library or not, the owl could be downright lazy sometimes. "Let me know if she needs our help, Jet."

"Yes, partner!" He took off, flying towards the balconies overlooking the ground floor. Three stories packed with shelves peered down at us, while a hidden fourth floor had gone missing years ago, and nobody had ever been able to find it since.

"The disrespect." Sylvester sniffed. "I shall take my leave."

He took off with a loud hoot, and I stepped back to avoid his wings clipping me in the face.

Estelle, meanwhile, tilted her head to look up at the balconies. "I hope she's okay."

"She usually is," I said. "There's nothing in here she can't handle."

In theory. As I lowered my gaze from the balconies, Aunt Candace cleared her throat loudly. My other aunt stood beside the reference shelves, her usual notebook and pen floating at her side. Another pen stuck out of her tangled red hair, and she wore a pair of eye-wateringly pink leggings.

"Hey, Aunt Candace," I said. "I thought you were busy writing."

"I found *this*—" She held up a wriggling wyrm by its tail— "in my *room*. It chewed several holes in my manuscript."

"What?" Aunt Candace's room wasn't anywhere near the place where Aunt Adelaide had found the other book-wyrm as far as I was aware. "Your sister found one in the returns box too."

"I won't have them destroying my work," she fumed. "I want them gone!"

"We'll have to wait for Aunt Adelaide," I said. "She went to take the book back to its shelf, but I don't know why it's taking her so long."

"I imagine that's obvious," she said. "She found more of them."

"What?" My heart sank, and when she made to return to the living quarters, I called her back. "Don't you want to help get rid of them? You don't want more of them getting into your research cave, do you?"

She gave me a withering look. "That's not necessary. I'll put a spell on the door to keep them out."

"That won't help the rest of the library." Not that that

would necessarily sway her to help us. "Come on. You're already downstairs. Unless you'd rather watch the front desk instead?"

"Certainly *not*."

"Or deal with the Unfinished Section?" Estelle suggested.

"That place is still there?" Aunt Candace wore an intrigued expression. "I thought you got rid of it."

"There's no getting rid of anything in here, as you well know," said Estelle.

I lifted my head when Jet came zipping back into view. "She's on the third floor, partner! The wyrms have infested a whole shelf!"

Oh no. "Where'd they even come from?"

"They breed in old books," said Estelle, her face falling. "It was probably one of the shipments we got in earlier this summer... though I really thought we checked them all for contamination."

"They're sneaky creatures," said Aunt Candace. "I wonder if I can incorporate them into my next book."

"If you don't help us get rid of them, that might end up being literal," I said. "Jet, how many of us does she need?"

"As many hands as possible!" he answered.

If Aunt Adelaide was struggling, the situation must be bad. "I can watch the desk... or ask Cass."

"Good luck with that," said Aunt Candace. "If you want a more efficient way to deal with those wyrms, you can always ask her to set her animals on them."

"Definitely not." Cass's menagerie of magical monsters was more likely to run around terrorising the public or eating the books themselves than to deal with our pest problem.

"She won't want to listen to us fighting book-wyrms either," Estelle said. "I'll see if I can convince her to come downstairs."

"Jet, can you stay here until then?" I asked the little crow, who chirped an affirmative. "Come on, Aunt Candace."

Estelle walked ahead towards the stairs, while Aunt Candace gave a dramatic sigh and then followed us. I was already having second thoughts; while my aunt was accomplished enough at magic, she was so absent-minded that having her around in a crisis ran the risk of her writing an account of said crisis in her notebook instead of doing anything to help. Her notebook and pen were a constant presence, floating at her side as we climbed the spiralling stairs.

At the third floor, Estelle made for the closed door that led to Cass's favoured corridor. I knew she kept a manticore in there, among other things, but the ominous scuttling noises in the background came from elsewhere.

As we approached the location of the noise, I pulled out my wand. While my Biblio-Witchery was more effective, I suspected I'd need at least one hand free. Seeing Aunt Candace attempt to sneak away, I waylaid her. "Come on, don't run off. We need your help."

"Why not ask her instead?" She jerked her head towards the open door to the Magical Creatures Division.

Cass stood with her customary scowl on her face, her red hair pulled into a topknot and her clothes as rough as one would expect of someone who spent her time on hands and knees, dealing with magical monsters.

"Be reasonable, Cass," Estelle was saying to her younger sister. "We need someone to watch the desk, and Sylvester has taken off in a sulk."

Cass pushed her glasses up the bridge of her nose. "Did Rory do something to annoy him?"

Well... yes, but that's not the point. Whenever we left the owl in the customer-facing side of the library, he inevitably caused trouble.

"Would you rather help with the wyrms?" asked Estelle. "They even got to Aunt Candace's books. There's no telling where they'll end up next."

At that moment, a loud crash sounded from elsewhere on the third floor, like a bookcase falling over. *Oh no.*

"Bet she's thrilled." Cass sighed. "Fine, I'll watch the desk, but you owe me."

"Thanks," Estelle said. "I'll pay you back by keeping the wyrms out of your animals' cages."

"That's no reward. In fact, you can feel free to feed them to my manticore if you want to risk opening the door to his cage."

"I'll pass, thanks."

While Cass left her corridor, I continued to move in the direction the crashing noise had come from. I kept my wand at the ready, one eye on Aunt Candace.

The wand had once been my dad's, though he'd given it up when he'd moved away from the magical world and had hidden it in the library. When I'd found the wand—or it had found me—I'd known the library was capable of far more than I'd realised. One would think that it wouldn't have an issue rejecting pests, but I guessed book-wyrms were one problem my grandmother hadn't foreseen when she'd designed the place.

I'd already faced murderous vampires, time-travelling werewolves straight out of my aunt's novels, and even a full-grown dragon. A few wyrms wouldn't be a problem. Right?

2

While Cass went down to the front desk, the rest of us prepared to face the infestation. Only Aunt Candace didn't seem particularly fazed by the ominous crashing noise we'd heard. Her notebook and pen continued to bounce along behind us as we walked past two patrons, who seemed oblivious to the chaos happening elsewhere on the third floor. One, a middle-aged witch, lay so far back in a hammock that I couldn't see her face, while a gangly shifter sat nearby, eating a giant sandwich.

"Hey!" Estelle said to the latter. "No eating in the library."

The shifter nearly dropped the sandwich. "Huh?"

"You know the rules, surely," she said. "Go outside to eat that."

He hastily picked up a book that was lying next to him. "I was reading a book."

His argument might have worked if he hadn't been holding the book upside down. I glimpsed the title—*Tips for Dealing with Abnormal Hair Growth*—and evidently, so did Aunt Candace, as she broke into peals of laughter.

"Might be a bit late for that." The smile slid off her face

when her attention fell on a stack of books near the hammock. "Is that one of my books? Someone has *turned down the page corners*. That is a crime against literature, that is."

Estelle grabbed Aunt Candace's arm as she made to march over to the hammock. "Calm down. We have a nest of book-wyrms to deal with, remember?"

Aunt Candace tugged her arm free with a disgruntled huff, but she did as Estelle told her to. We left the two patrons behind and continued towards the site of the book-wyrm infestation.

"Is it just me, or have the shelves moved around since the last time I came up here?" I asked Estelle.

"Probably," she said. "They do that."

That was true enough. The library's general layout always stayed the same, but parts of it had a flexible rela-tionship with the laws of space-time. Sometimes, book-shelves got bored and wandered from between one floor and the next, doors changed locations every other day, and whole sections vanished outright for weeks at a time. This time, I was sure the third floor had acquired some new padlocked doors that could only be accessed by anyone carrying one of our family's handmade keys. I hadn't been given a key of my own yet, since the rooms behind those doors often contained threats that required advanced magic to deal with.

When we passed yet another row of padlocked doors, I looked more closely and realised we'd walked in a full circle around the third floor without finding Aunt Adelaide or the book-wyrms.

"Has the infestation upset the library?" I stopped in my tracks when a bloodcurdling shriek came from nearby. "That wasn't a book-wyrm. Please tell me Cass locked the door to her manticore's cage."

"She did," said Estelle. "I watched her do it. That wasn't an animal."

"It came from the Magical Creatures Division, though." *That* door had stayed where it was, recognisable by the sign that said "Staff Only beyond This Point. Watch Out for the Chimera." "The chimera didn't get out, did it?"

"No…" Estelle surveyed the shelves, her brow pinched. "Let me see… I think it's this way."

A second howl punctuated her words, and I winced. "What *was* that if not a monster?"

"A book?" suggested Aunt Candace.

The books in the Magical Creatures Division were certainly a tad more talkative than one might expect, but they mostly communicated in grunts and growls, not screams. And occasionally tried to bite one's fingers off. Some of them were covered in fur, while others had teeth and claws and were contained within cages or shelves covered in glass—or hidden behind sealed doors marked with *X* symbols to indicate that nobody was to go inside except for one of us.

We rounded a corner, and Estelle reached into a cubbyhole between the shelves and pulled out some gloves. "Just in case."

"Thanks." I took the pair of gloves she offered me and looked for my aunt, but she'd vanished. "Ah—Aunt Candace?"

"She must have run off." Estelle tutted, pulling on her own gloves. "I knew bringing her up here was a bad idea."

Another shriek echoed from ahead. I hastened to put on my gloves as I followed Estelle through the stacks.

Chaos met us on the other side. A large bookcase lay across our path, the contents spilling out onto the floor, while Aunt Adelaide stood amid the chaos, struggling to keep her grip on a large book. *Aunt Candace was right.* The book was screaming, its pages gnashing like teeth as it howled and raged, while dozens more books lay scattered around the floor. Some were inert, but others were moving, crawling across the floor or shuffling in a crab-like manner, depending on whether they had claws or the means of propelling themselves along. *Oh no.*

"There you are," Aunt Adelaide puffed out, wrangling the shrieking book. "I was starting to wonder where you'd got to."

"The library rearranged things again." Estelle ran to pick up one of the runaway books, holding its spine carefully between her gloved fingers. "Where should I put it?"

"In here." Aunt Adelaide indicated a stack of boxes behind her, while I ran to grab a book myself—opting to start with one that didn't have teeth. "Where's that owl?"

"He went off in a sulk," I said. "Sorry. It was my fault."

"No, it wasn't." Estelle ran after another book. "He was probably looking for an excuse—ouch!" When she'd reached for the book, its pages had clamped onto her upper arm like claws.

"Let me help." I hurried to her side and cast a freeze-frame spell on the book. The two of us managed to pry it from her arm, and then she carried it to a box in the corner.

When the book in Aunt Adelaide's hands let out another ear-blistering scream, I cast a freeze-frame spell on that one too.

"Thanks, Rory," she said breathlessly. "Can you help me repair it? That might stop the screaming."

"Sure." I reached for my Biblio-Witch Inventory and flipped to the most recent page while she gingerly held the book open. Glad I'd taken the time to learn the spell earlier, I tapped the word *repair*, and the gaping hole in the pages vanished.

"Thanks, Rory." She closed the book. "I'll fix the shelves. Can you and Estelle round up the other books?"

"Sure." Unfortunately, the books had scattered in all directions at the first taste of freedom, and the library's rearrangement of the third floor hadn't helped matters either. "Let me know if you need my—"

The book in her arms unfroze and promptly began screaming again. I covered my ears and then tripped backwards over a furred book that was in the middle of an escape attempt. "Whoa."

"Careful," Aunt Adelaide warned as I caught my balance and seized the escaping book. "Can you check for any damaged pages?"

"Sure." I opened the runaway book, revealing several rows of fangs. Glad of the gloves, I gingerly turned the pages, the other book's screams echoing in my ears. "Should I cast a soundproofing spell?"

"No, it'll only get more distressed—oh, don't put all the ones with teeth in the same box," she added, indicating the stack of boxes next to the fallen bookshelf. "Grab one with a sealable lid."

"Will do." I dropped the furred book into a box and closed the lid then went in pursuit of another. In the general chaos, I couldn't even see where the book-wyrms were hiding—except inside the shelves that had collapsed, evidently. They must have eaten straight through the wood.

"Thanks, Rory," said Aunt Adelaide as I brought several more books back and sorted them into boxes. "I'll get these shelves repaired while you and Estelle hunt down the books."

"Sounds good." Aunt Candace remained absent, but given her track record, it was to be expected that she'd decided to hide in the background and take notes rather than helping.

I found Estelle in an alcove, trying to fish another book

out of a tank full of books—presumably waterproof—and which had… fins? "What's this, the aquatic division?"

"Yes, these are waterproof books," said Estelle. "For merpeople and the like, you know."

I blinked. "Book-wyrms can't swim, can they?"

"No, but this book isn't supposed to be here." She used a claw-like instrument to grasp the book and lift it out of the water. "Gotcha."

I ducked when the book shook itself like a dog, splattering both of us with water. "This is going to take some cleaning up."

"No kidding." Estelle carried the book out of the alcove and picked up another box to toss it into. "We're going to run out of boxes."

"Your mum's repairing the damaged shelf," I explained. "That should make things easier. It's hard to keep the books contained when they keep trying to eat one another."

"You aren't wrong." She waved her wand over the book, drying its damp pages, and then closed the lid on the box. "Does she want us to round up the rest while she deals with the shelves?"

"Yeah." I spotted another book scuttling away through a door, and as I reached out to grab its spine, it sprouted several tentacles. "Whoa."

Estelle swore. "I think that one came from the tank when I took off the lid."

"Figures." I reached for my wand as the book began crawling up the wall. "Hang on."

I freeze-framed the book, locking it in place. When I strode to retrieve it, though, I found its tentacles had locked to the wall. A tug-of-war ensued before I managed to pry it free and then tossed it back into the tank.

"I hope that's the only one that got out." Estelle shut the lid on the tank. "Now for the rest of the escapees."

"I hope none of them got through any of the locked doors."

"They shouldn't have been able to," she said, "but these books can be surprisingly wily. Best not to open any doors that aren't already open, in my mind."

"Good call." I backed out of the alcove and spied a tunnel-like entrance to another part of the library, from which I could hear a series of distinct rustling noises. "I swear I've never seen half of these rooms before."

"Of all the places the book-wyrms had to infest," said Estelle, "it had to be the part of the library where the books can walk."

"Maybe they made friends with the books."

"I doubt it." She gave a laugh. "The wyrms prefer eating the books to befriending them. I only hope they left Cass's room alone."

"Maybe you should have asked her to help instead of Aunt Candace. I don't even know where she went."

"Typical." She walked through the tunnel, where we found a book scuttling across the ceiling in a crab-like manner.

When I reached up, its pages morphed into claws and latched on to my arm. "Ow."

"Keep still." Estelle fired a spell that caused the book's grip to loosen before it could puncture my skin. "Aunt Candace tried to label this section 'Gripping Reads,' but my mum shot the idea down."

"I'm surprised these haven't featured in a book of hers." I held the book at arm's length while I carried it to a box and tossed it in.

"True," said Estelle. "She prefers her research to be hands-on, but not if it involves *losing* a hand."

When we'd finished searching the tunnel, I realised the screaming book had finally gone silent. Estelle and I carried the books we'd retrieved out of the Magical Creatures Division and found that Aunt Adelaide had managed to repair the damage to the bookcase and was stacking books onto the newly repaired shelves.

"Thanks, both of you." She helped us carry over the books we'd recaptured and set about putting them back on the shelves. "I checked, and none of the books seem to have made it through the secured doors… or into Cass's room either."

"Oh, good," said Estelle. "I mean, we could have asked Cass to get them out if they did, but not if one of her pets ate the books. There's only so much a repair spell can do."

"Exactly," said Aunt Adelaide. "Now the shelves are intact, it should be easier to see which are missing. It'd be nice if Candace offered a helping hand, but I assume she's still working on her book."

"We did bring her upstairs with us," I said. "I guess she wasn't that committed, even though a book-wyrm ate a hole in the page of her manuscript."

"It didn't, did it?" Aunt Adelaide groaned under her breath. "*Where* they came from in the first place…"

"Have you made sure there aren't any more inside the shelves?" asked Estelle.

"Yes, they're all in there." Aunt Adelaide indicated a bucket full of wriggling wyrms. "Sylvester will get to feast on them later."

"He hasn't even earned it," I said. "Though we might be able to use them as bait to lure him back upstairs."

"Good call." Estelle reached for the bucket. "I think we'll need more than three pairs of hands. Not that Sylvester actually has hands, but still."

We had a lot of missing books to find and repair, so I got to work hunting down the rest. Since we'd found the ones in the immediate vicinity, I headed farther afield, to the area where we'd seen the two unwitting patrons on our way past. Neither was there any longer, but Aunt Candace sat in the hammock that had been occupied by the witch, rocking gently back and forth.

"What're you doing?" I called to her. "Aunt Candace?"

Where were her notebook and pen? She stared into the distance, and when she spotted me, an expression of vague confusion crossed her face. "Oh, hello. Who are you?"

"Rory." I studied her face, trying to gauge if she was joking or not. "Your niece. What're you doing up here?"

"Honestly, I… I'm not quite sure." She rose to her feet, the hammock swaying behind her. "Rory, you say? Strange name."

"It's short for Aurora, and you knew that, since you're my aunt." She might have been a decent actress, but her weirdly blank expression looked too convincing. Had someone cast a spell on her?

Delight spread across her face. "I'm an aunt? I always wanted to be an aunt."

"Well, I have great news. You're an aunt three times over." If she'd fallen under a spell, she had an excuse for not helping us out, but I didn't have a clue how she'd ended up in this state. "Can you wait there a moment?"

If she was faking it, she'd get bored soon enough, and Estelle was better equipped to deal with this kind of situation than I was. I retraced my steps and caught up to my cousin near the aquatic room. "Estelle, I need backup."

"Not another book-wyrm?"

"Not exactly. Aunt Candace has forgotten who I am."

"What?" Estelle followed my gaze over to the shelves where I'd left Aunt Candace. "Is she making a ploy for attention?"

"I wondered, but she's not even writing, which seems

unlike her." I led the way to our aunt, who'd returned to her hammock and had resumed rocking back and forth.

"Aunt Candace?" Estelle called to her. "Are you okay?"

"I really am an aunt three times over?" She smiled up at us. "Where's the third one?"

Estelle and I exchanged bewildered glances. *She doesn't even remember Cass?* "Downstairs. Your sister is here, though."

"I have a sister too?" Her delighted expression intensified. "I always wanted one of those."

"She really didn't," Estelle whispered in my ear. "She's always said she wished she was an only child."

"Oh, fun," I said. "She's forgotten all of us. Does she know her *own* name?"

"Good question," said Estelle. "I'll take care of her while you find my mum, okay?"

"Thanks." My cousin was better at handling a crisis than I was, especially one that involved a wayward spell of some kind. Had one of the books been responsible? It certainly wouldn't have surprised me if there was a book that made people instantly lose their memories, though it was rare for them to affect members of my family.

I tracked down Aunt Adelaide near the repaired bookcase. "Aunt Candace has lost her memories."

"She hasn't, has she?" she said. "How'd she manage that?"

"Estelle is trying to find out, but it seems genuine." I spied Estelle guiding our aunt through the shelves towards us. "Can the book-wyrms eat a hole in someone's brain?"

I was only half joking. Aunt Candace might as well have lost her personality as well as her memories—and where were her notebook and pen?

"No, of course not," said Aunt Adelaide. "Did she open any of the doors?"

"Good question." The spell was more likely to have come from behind one of the high-security doors than from an escaped book, though it was beyond me to figure out which it might have been. "I'll ask."

I strode over to Aunt Candace. "Ah—did you open any doors?"

"Doors?" she echoed. "Yes… over there."

I swivelled on my heel, following her gaze, and Estelle gasped. Beyond the shelves was a door that hadn't been there before as far as I knew. Granted, a whole host of new doors had appeared recently, but I was pretty sure I'd remember one that was bright purple. It lay partly open, so I walked closer, trying to get a better look inside.

"Stop." Aunt Adelaide held out a hand. "Don't go in there, Rory."

"Why?"

"Because," she said, "that's the door to the missing fourth-floor corridor."

"That's the missing corridor?" The purple door was undeniably real, but why had it chosen now to reappear? Hadn't it been gone—invisible, if not vanished outright—for decades?

Aunt Candace came bounding forward and grabbed Aunt Adelaide's hands. "You're my sister, are you? I always wanted one of those."

Aunt Adelaide's bewildered expression might have made me laugh if it hadn't been for the bombshell her sister had dropped. "No, you didn't, Candace. You *do* remember your own name, don't you?"

"Of course I do." She snorted. "Don't be ridiculous."

"Where's your notebook and pen?"

"My what?"

"Your notebook and pen," I repeated. "The ones you use to write your books."

No way. She hadn't forgotten she was an author, had she?

"I write *books*?" Delight lit up her face. "Are they good?"

"Erm…" What was I supposed to say to that? I'd never actually read one of her books all the way through, but I wasn't her target audience, and I also knew how sensitive she was to criticism. "Yes. They're very popular."

Better to be safe than sorry. She might not remember her own novels, but I preferred to avoid upsetting her.

"Yes, they are." Aunt Adelaide firmly released her sister's hands. "You were in the middle of working on a new project recently, in fact."

"Interesting." Aunt Candace's expression turned to a vague smile. "I wonder why I forgot."

"I can help you remember what they are." Aunt Adelaide reached into her pocket and pulled over her wand. "Just keep still for a moment."

"You're putting a spell on me?"

"No, we're taking it off," said Estelle. "Ah—*do* you remember anyone casting a spell on you?"

"No, I can't say I do." She looked perturbed. "Another jealous writer, were they?"

Aunt Adelaide gave a flick of her wand, and a bright flash of light made us all close our eyes for an instant. "How do you feel now?"

I opened my eyes, and Aunt Candace's vague smile remained intact. "I feel great. Thanks for asking."

Okay, that definitely didn't work.

"Let me try this." Aunt Adelaide pulled out her Biblio-Witch Inventory and opened it then tapped on a few words. Each caused a wave of static that made the hairs on my arms stand on end, but Aunt Candace remained unaffected.

"What is that?" she asked. "I've never seen that kind of magic before."

Estelle pulled out her own Biblio-Witch Inventory. "Let's see if it works better with two of us at once."

I figured that the words weren't ones I'd learned yet, but if Aunt Adelaide hadn't been able to undo the spell, the odds of me being able to lend a hand were low. Even when Estelle joined in, their combined efforts didn't do much more than conjure up a few sparks that Aunt Candace tried to catch in her hands.

"Word magic, is it?" she asked. "Can you teach me to do that too?"

"Maybe later," Estelle evaded. "Mum, I think that's all we have."

"We've tried all the common reversal spells," Aunt Adelaide said in an undertone. "Let's try some of the less common ones."

They put away their Biblio-Witch Inventories and pulled out their wands again. I hadn't known there were so many variations on a reversal spell, but Aunt Candace retained the same vague expression no matter what the others did.

Finally, Aunt Adelaide lowered her wand. "It's a powerful hex or a curse, I'm guessing, so we'll need something more specialised... and to know where it came from."

I indicated the vibrant purple door across from us. "It must have come from in there, right? We don't have to go inside, but we can have a look around."

"Nobody has been there since your grandmother died," said Aunt Adelaide. "It's too risky."

Aunt Candace gasped. "Our mother is dead?"

"You remember her?" Estelle asked.

"No... no, I can't say I do." A frown wrinkled her brow. "How strange."

"And do you remember the library?" Estelle pressed. "That's where we are."

"A library?" Understanding dawned on Aunt Candace's face. "I wondered why there were so many books in here. Can you give me a tour?"

"Later." Aunt Adelaide stepped in front of her sister. "We'll go downstairs and start with the ground floor."

"Are you sure that's a good idea?" whispered Estelle.

"It's safer downstairs," said Aunt Adelaide. "And it's worth seeing if it makes a difference if she's away from the door. Both of you—I can trust you to stay here without going inside, can't I?"

"Of course." Curiosity burned inside me, and I was willing to bet Estelle felt the same, but she and I both knew better than to mess around with the library's unknown corridor. Losing our memories was nowhere near the worst of all the possible outcomes if we went through that door.

Aunt Adelaide led Aunt Candace away, while Estelle and I remained outside the door to the fourth-floor corridor. Despite myself, I moved a little closer, noting that its colouring appeared more ruby red than purple. Through a narrow gap, I could see only darkness, with nothing to indicate what lay on the other side.

"Where did the door even come from?" I turned to Estelle. "Did it just appear out of nowhere?"

"I don't know." Estelle's expression clouded. "I mean, Aunt Candace might have been the one who found it. It's just like her to figure out how to find the corridor herself without telling the rest of us."

"True." Aunt Candace's insatiable sense of curiosity got her into trouble on a not-infrequent basis, but there was something weird about the whole situation. Why had the corridor picked now to reappear and not ten years earlier? "How, though?"

"Don't ask me. I know even less than she does." Estelle tilted her head to see through the gap in the door. "This might account for why the third floor's shelves have been moving around all morning. I did wonder."

"It has an effect on the rest of the library?" Alarm rose inside me. "Wait, do you think the curse on Aunt Candace might be able to spread to other people too?"

"No," she said. "Curses are usually cast on a specific location, so she touched either the door or something on the other side."

"Honestly." I shook my head. "Even by her standards, that's reckless."

"I know," she said. "I wouldn't have thought she'd walk into a curse on purpose, but perhaps she couldn't resist."

"Then we need to make sure nobody else does the same." I peered at the door to see if it had any marks that indicated how it'd cursed Aunt Candace, but aside from its odd colour, it looked to be made of ordinary wood. "If the door is cursed, how do we close it?"

"With these." She held up her hands, which were encased in the gloves she'd been wearing to handle the biting books. "Most cursed objects require direct skin contact to work. I should be fine."

"I hope you're right." I tensed when she tentatively reached for the door with one hand, ready to intervene if she got into trouble—though I frankly had no idea what might come out of the corridor. The library, without fail, went out of its way to surprise me at every turn.

Estelle's fingers closed around the door handle, and she pushed it shut. The door clicked into place, and after a short pause, she took a step back. "That seems to be fine."

"You remember who I am, don't you?" I asked warily.

"Yeah—like I said, the gloves keep out any curses." She turned her back on the door. "Ideally, we need to make sure nobody else touches it, though I'm more inclined to think the curse came from somewhere inside. The door doesn't have a key, though, and I'm not sure it can be magically sealed so nobody else can get in. Not without locking ourselves out in the process."

"Your mum might know." I moved towards the stairs. "I don't know if we should leave it unattended..."

"One of us should stay here," she agreed. "I don't *think* it'll disappear again, but you never know."

"I'm more concerned that something'll get *out*. We're near Cass's corridor, after all." My curiosity remained intact, but I was under no illusions as to who was the more accomplished at magic out of the pair of us. "Want to stay here while I go downstairs and ask your mum for advice?"

"Of course," she said. "Don't worry. I won't touch the door again."

"I know." My gaze travelled over its burnished red surface. "It disappeared when you were a kid, right? Did you see it before then?"

"No," she replied. "I was only a few months old, and Mum didn't bring me up here when I was a baby. Too many hazards."

"The same year Grandma died," I surmised. "She hid it before her death?"

"Honestly, I've never been able to get a straight answer on that one." Her lips pursed. "Mum doesn't remember. She was a new parent at the time, and she spent most of her time taking care of me, not paying attention to Grandma's bizarre experiments."

"Until she died," I surmised. "I guess Aunt Candace might have paid closer attention than she did, but we won't know for sure until we get that curse off her."

Given the dangers of the third floor, I probably didn't want to know what might be lurking up on the fourth... but how and why had Grandma hidden it? And why had it turned on Aunt Candace? Yes, not everything in the library was controllable or even understandable, but it was through Grandma Hawthorn that our family had inherited our ability to draw magic out of words in the first place.

In the meantime, I left Estelle to watch the door and followed Aunt Adelaide's path downstairs. When I reached the ground floor, I saw her coaxing Aunt Candace into a seat in the Reading Corner, to the evident confusion of the nearby patrons sitting in its beanbags and hammocks. I'd forgotten there were other patrons in here… which was why we'd left Cass in charge of the desk. Oops. Hoping she hadn't bitten anyone's head off, I went to speak to my aunt first.

"Nobody else is cursed, are they?" I asked Aunt Adelaide.

"Not as far as I'm aware," she said. "Where's Estelle? Still on the third floor?"

"Yeah. I figured someone ought to keep an eye on that door," I explained. "We closed it, but we need to make sure nobody else walks inside."

"You closed the door?"

"Estelle did—with her gloves on," I amended. "She said it was fine, but since there's no lock…"

"I had already intended to bar off the third floor for everyone except our family until the book-wyrms are dealt with," she said. "If we put a repelling spell on the stairs, that ought to stop anyone from walking up there by accident."

"Good idea," I said. "Estelle suggested that we ought to have someone keeping an eye out to make sure it doesn't disappear again, since we don't know how it reappeared to begin with."

Her forehead creased. "I have some ideas, but you're right… we shouldn't leave the corridor unattended until we understand why it came back."

"Ideas?" I glanced at Aunt Candace. "She found it herself, right? And didn't tell us?"

"That's what I'm assuming." She drew in a breath. "As to the curse, I'm inclined to think my sister must have stepped through the door and walked into some kind of defensive measure our mother put in place."

My aunt sat on a beanbag, her shoulders hunched and her expression so bewildered that I almost felt sorry for her. "Has she mentioned anything about what she saw in there?"

"No, she doesn't remember a thing," Adelaide said. "I tried asking a range of questions, but it's a powerful curse, and not one I've seen before."

"Defensive, you said." I thought back to my conversation with Estelle. "Why would Grandma put a curse that dangerous on her corridor?"

"For reasons of security—but Candace is family. I don't know why she was affected."

"Are you talking about me?" Aunt Candace gave her sister an aggrieved stare. "I can hear you. You think I did something to your door, do you?"

"We just want to find out what happened to you," I told her. "That's why we're asking questions."

"I'm the victim here," she said. "I didn't curse myself, did I?"

Possibly. It wouldn't have been the weirdest thing she'd done in the name of research, but in her current state, it was hard to say. I had a hard time believing that anyone else could have found the door, let alone managed to get it open.

"One of us should probably check on Cass," said Aunt Adelaide. "To make sure she's doing her job."

"And tell her about the curse." Knowing her, she'd find it hilarious that our aunt had lost her memories, though she might not be as thrilled that the corridor had reappeared right next to her own favoured corner of the library.

Leaving my aunts in the Reading Corner, I went to the front desk. Cass was reading a paperback—one of Aunt Candace's—and looked up when I approached. "Got rid of the infestation?"

"Not exactly," I said. "We fixed the damage, but we didn't find the nest. Aunt Candace somehow got herself cursed, so now we have another issue on our hands."

"You took *her* with you?"

"Yes," I said, "and she found the missing corridor to the fourth floor."

"Found it?" she said. "I was starting to think it was one of her jokes."

"Nope. It's real, and it's put a curse on Aunt Candace that caused her to lose her memories."

"Well, that ought to make her a little less annoying for a bit."

I blinked. "Aren't you worried? She's even forgotten she's a writer. Also, she's delighted at the idea that she has three nieces and is excited to meet you."

Cass burst out laughing. "Priceless. Watch the desk while I go and 'meet' her, will you?"

"Cass, seriously…" I trailed off when the door opened, and Xavier walked in.

The blond Reaper didn't look like someone who escorted the dead into the afterlife for a living despite wearing all black, and his aquamarine eyes were pure bewilderment when he saw Cass doubled over in laughter.

"Hey, Rory," he said. "Ah—what's going on?"

"Aunt Candace lost her memories," I explained. "She found the missing corridor to the fourth floor…"

"There's a fourth floor?"

"There was before Grandma lost it. Or turned it invisible." I turned to Cass, who kept snickering. "This isn't funny. Your mother tried every single reversal spell in her Biblio-Witch Inventory and outside of it and still didn't manage to remove the curse from Aunt Candace. She thinks it's a defensive measure our grandmother cast on the corridor."

"I expect she's right," Cass said. "And it's just like Aunt Candace to walk straight into it."

"At least it doesn't seem to have affected anyone except

her," I said, "but she's family, so why would it treat her like an outsider?"

"Don't ask me. I wasn't even born when the corridor disappeared." She shrugged. "Lighten up, Rory. At least she was the one who got cursed and not someone more important."

"And what if she isn't the last?" Worry bled into my voice. "We don't know what's behind that door and what it might be capable of."

We didn't even know how Aunt Candace had found it—or if it might disappear again, taking any chance of curing her along with it.

"Really?" Xavier asked. "She's just lost her memories? Nothing else?"

"Yeah, and the curse is powerful enough that my aunt can't remove it," I said. "We aren't sure if the curse came from the door itself or from something behind it, since Aunt Candace can't remember anything."

"I can come up and take a look," he offered. "I'm immune to curses."

"Are you?" That made sense given that he was technically undead, but my skin prickled at the notion of him walking into that corridor. "Estelle closed the door, but I guess it didn't harm any of us when it was open before."

"Good luck with that," Cass said. "Curses are invisible. Sending a Reaper in there isn't going to help you find the source."

"If Xavier looks around, he might be able to find out what Grandma actually put in there." I didn't like the idea of him going into a potentially dangerous corner of the library, either, but it was that or go in there myself and end up cursed—or Estelle or Aunt Adelaide. Cass certainly wouldn't volunteer.

"Fine," she said. "Do as you like."

Surprised she'd given in so readily, Xavier and I headed for the stairs.

"How's your boss?" I asked him.

"His usual self," he said. "Grumpy, reaping souls, being antisocial. Did I hear you had another book-wyrm incident?"

"Yeah. That's how we ended up on the third floor." I gave him a brief overview of the situation as we climbed the staircase. "I know we shouldn't have taken Aunt Candace with us, but she was complaining that a book-wyrm chewed a hole in her book, and I figured she should make herself useful for once."

"She must have already been looking for the corridor," he remarked, "for it to have reappeared so quickly."

"True, but without her memories, we don't have any eyewitnesses who saw what really happened up here."

"Nobody else saw?"

"Not that I know of." I thought back to the two patrons we'd seen earlier, but I hadn't thought to look for them downstairs. "We'll check on that later."

At the third floor, the door remained under Estelle's watchful eye, its wooden surface glowing faintly orange.

"Did it change colour?" I asked her.

"Yeah, it did." Her eyes widened in surprise when she saw Xavier approaching. "Did you bring him to look around?"

"Yeah—Reapers are immune to curses, so he offered to check out the corridor," I explained. "I don't know if he'll be able to get very far, but it's better than another one of us ending up cursed."

"Oh, good idea," she said. "I didn't think of that. Though— I mean, Xavier, do you really want to get involved in our mess?"

"It's fine," he said. "I don't mind. It's a lot more interesting than staying at home with my boss."

"All right, then." She stepped back from the door. "You'd

better open it yourself. I don't *think* the door itself is cursed, but you never know."

"Good call." Xavier approached the door, reaching for the handle. My breath caught. From the back, he didn't look like a Reaper at all. He looked human and vulnerable, and it almost made me want to jump in and intervene to stop him from going in.

As if he'd sensed my thoughts, he turned back to me and nodded, a reassuring gesture. I smiled back, pushing my doubts aside.

Then he opened the door and walked in.

4

As Xavier disappeared into the corridor beyond the door, I held my breath instinctively. For a moment, all was silent.

"Ah, Xavier?" I called out. "Everything okay?"

"Yeah… there's nothing here but a staircase," came his reply.

"The fourth floor," Estelle put in. "The stairs lead up there… are you sure there isn't anything else, Xavier?"

"Nothing, at least down here," he said. "Want me to go up?"

"All right," I said. "You don't see anything that looks suspicious?"

"Nothing." I heard his soft footsteps climbing the stairs. "This place seems pretty empty."

"What's upstairs?" I listened for each footstep, and there was a pause when he reached the top. "Can you see?"

"Not much," he replied. "Just a corridor… a bit like your living quarters."

"Are there any doors?" asked Estelle.

"A few. I can't see the end of the corridor—it goes around

a corner." More footsteps interspersed his words, and his voice grew fainter as he moved farther away.

Unable to bear the tension a moment longer, I found myself moving closer to the orange door, but even when I angled my head so that I could see through the crack between door and wall, there was nothing to see. "Xavier—are any of the doors open?"

"Yes—and there's someone else up here."

"Who?" My heart gave a lurch. "A person?"

"No, a wolf," he replied. "Weird. There's a room full of ceiling-high mirrors, and this guy—I assume he's a werewolf—seems to be stuck in the middle of them."

"Are you sure it's not a trap?" Estelle asked dubiously. "Is the guy definitely alive?"

Wait. "Did that shifter who was sitting down here go through the door? The guy with the sandwich?"

Estelle clapped her hands to her mouth. "He might have. Oh no."

"Xavier, can you get him out of there?" I didn't exactly relish the idea of Xavier risking himself, but no level of magical trap could compete with his Reaper abilities. "How'd he get stuck?"

"I think he's confused about which way is out because of all the mirrors," he replied. "I can help him, but he doesn't realise I'm here, and I know shifters can get a little panicky when they're cornered."

Especially by a Reaper, I'm betting. "We can't leave him in there, though. Can you try to get him out of the room?"

"Sure." A few indistinct thudding noises followed and then a loud howl.

I tensed, ready to run and help if necessary, but Estelle shook her head in warning, and I stilled. "Xavier, are you okay?"

"Yeah," Xavier called out. "I'll be down in a second."

More howling and thudding followed, and through the gap in the door, I saw Xavier descending the stairs—while struggling to keep hold of the wriggling and panicking shifter. Being a Reaper, Xavier was stronger than he looked, but when he reached the door, the shifter yelped and broke free from his grip. I stepped aside as the werewolf pelted across the floor and behind a bookshelf.

"Sorry." Xavier walked out of the room. "Carrying him was the only way to get him downstairs. He kept running in circles and panicking."

"Maybe he thought you were going to take his soul." I peered around the bookshelf and confirmed that it was definitely the same shifter as before, as evidenced from the fact that he was currently in the form of a human again. And naked. Werewolves left their clothes behind when they shifted, so he must have left them upstairs.

The shifter flushed bright red when he saw us looking at him. "Where are my clothes?"

Estelle strode over. "What were you doing up there? Wait —you do remember who you are, don't you?"

"What?" He grabbed the shelf to pull himself to his feet and then jumped violently when one of the books started hissing at him. "Is that a trick question?"

"No," said Estelle. "You shouldn't have been in that corridor."

"Oh." His flush deepened. "Sorry. I didn't know. I'd never seen that door before…"

"But you do remember where you are?" Estelle pressed.

"The library," he mumbled. "I'm sorry."

Evidently, he hadn't lost his memory, unlike Aunt Candace, but why hadn't he been affected in the same way that she had? "Did you see anyone else upstairs?"

"No, but I heard noises," he mumbled. "The door was already open, so I figured it was okay to go in."

"You should still know better than to walk through unknown doors in a magical library," Estelle told him. "You're lucky it wasn't worse."

"There's also this." Xavier walked over, holding up a half-eaten sandwich. "I assume it's yours."

"Yes." The shifter caught the sandwich in his hands when Xavier tossed it to him. "I must've dropped it when I shifted."

"You were looking for somewhere to sneak off and eat that, weren't you?" I asked. "You're lucky you only ended up stuck in a room of mirrors. Did you look in any of the other rooms?"

He shook his head. "No. That was the first door I saw."

"It was the first door up there," Xavier ventured. "None of the others were open."

That suggested the shifter was telling the truth, but why had Aunt Candace been the one to lose her memories?

"Are you sure there wasn't anyone else upstairs?" I asked. "Did you see my aunt at all? She was with Estelle and me earlier…"

"I don't think so," he mumbled. "The first thing I did was look in that room, and seeing all those mirrors freaked me out."

"Was that when you shifted into animal form?" asked Estelle.

"Yes, and I lost my clothes…"

"Here." Xavier tossed a bundle of fabric at him. "That's all I found up there. I didn't try the other doors, but I can go back and have another look around."

"Not yet." As the shifter vanished behind the shelves to put his clothes back on, I whispered, "Is he telling the truth, do you think?"

"What he said was accurate to everything I saw up there," he said in an undertone. "The other doors were untouched, and it's possible he got so startled by the mirrors that he didn't look to see if anyone else was around?"

"Why didn't he lose his memory?"

"Aunt Candace might have looked behind a different door," he suggested. "He stopped at the first one."

The shifter reappeared, fully dressed, his expression mingling contrition and confusion. "I really am sorry. If you want me to leave…"

"I'll escort you to the door," Estelle said. "Rory, Xavier, do you want to stay up here?"

"Sure," I replied. "Xavier can have another look, but I don't know that he'll be able to open the locked doors…"

"Oh, that reminds me." She reached into her pocket and pulled out a key. "Try this. It's one of the one-size-fits-all keys for our top-security doors and usually only works for our family members, but I don't think we want any more casualties of the memory spell, do you?"

"No." I took the key and passed it to Xavier. "It's worth trying to see if this can unlock any of the doors."

I hadn't been entrusted with one of those keys yet, but I didn't have any envy towards Xavier for getting there first. Reapers didn't usually *need* a key to open an unlocked door, but even Reapers had their limits, and they couldn't use their shadow-walking powers to get into places they'd never seen before.

"Thanks," Xavier said to Estelle, and she departed with the shifter trailing behind her. "Not very bright, that one, is he?"

"No, but his memories are still intact," I replied. "Unlike my aunt's."

"For now."

"I guess the effects might come on later," I acknowledged, "but timed curses normally work the same way on all their targets."

"Then your aunt might have touched something the shifter didn't," he said. "Like those books you told me about. Ones that erase the memory of anyone who reads them."

"*Did* you see any books up there?"

"You know, I didn't." His brow creased. "Strange, for a library, but maybe they're behind some of the locked doors. Or maybe the corridor looked empty to me because I'm not from the library. I can't unlock its secrets."

"Not sure the rest of us can either," I murmured. "Even my aunts. Grandma hid that corridor well."

"She didn't leave any clues behind?"

"Nothing that my aunts have been able to figure out," I replied. "Or… well, it's possible that Aunt Candace did figure out where it was hidden and then decided not to tell anyone else. In fact, that's almost certainly why it showed up now after so many years of being missing."

"Sounds like her," he commented. "But while she's lost her memory, it's going to be hard to work out how she found it."

"That's the problem." I gave the door another scan. Its colour had changed again, from burnished orange to a deep sunset yellow. "The corridor might change its appearance too. I'm pretty sure it's the reason the third floor has been rearranging itself all morning. There's no telling what other security measures might be on the place."

"Fun," he said. "The room with the mirrors struck me as a possible security mechanism, but I wouldn't have tripped any alarms. My Reaper magic is designed for stealth, and according to most security systems, I don't really count as a person."

Despite the nervousness gnawing at my chest, I gave a mock frown. "That's a bit unfair."

He smiled. "Nah, it's easier that way. But in situations like this, it's a bit of a pain. There could have been a dozen alarms up there, and I wouldn't have known."

"So unless one of us volunteers to be a guinea pig…" I trailed off, thinking back to when I'd first seen the sandwich-eating shifter. "There was another patron upstairs when we were dealing with the book-wyrms. I hope she didn't get lost in there as well."

"I didn't see anyone else," he said, "but I'll test the key on the doors and see if anyone else has run into a trap."

"All right." As little as I liked the idea of Xavier going back into that corridor, we needed answers.

"I'll be back before you know it." He disappeared behind the door again, while I held my breath, listening for his soft footfalls on the stairs.

"Anything?" I called after a few moments of silence punctuated by the faint click of a key in a lock.

"No," he called back from above. "I tried the key on the second door, but it won't open."

"Ah." *I bet they only open for members of our family.* Which was a problem if the corridor was also designed to curse anyone who it perceived as a trespasser. "Try a couple more, then we'll think of something else."

"Sure thing." More footfalls and clicking sounds ensued, and within a couple of minutes, he reappeared through the door.

I held out a hand for the key. "I wonder if Aunt Candace is the one who opened the door to the mirror room."

"Might be," he commented as I put the key into my pocket. "If that triggered the curse, it might have only reacted to the first person to enter."

"That's a possibility." But it begged the question of why the curse hadn't recognised her as family. "I wish Grandma had left us with some ideas, but she didn't even leave a map of the library itself, let alone its missing corridor. And I'm not sure if it'll disappear again if we leave it unattended either."

"I can watch the door if you want to return that key to your cousin," he replied. "Though I probably don't count as family… or a person."

"You're a person to me." I gave him a smile. "But if the door vanishes for another decade and leaves us with no way to undo the spell on Aunt Candace, it's not ideal. Granted, Cass thinks it's an improvement, but it's downright weird for our aunt to have no idea she's a writer."

"Would the key work if your aunt Candace went back into the corridor?" he asked.

"It might, but we don't want her to get cursed twice over," I said. "Really, of all the times for Sylvester to disappear. He flew off in a sulk earlier."

"I bet he'd come back if he knew what was going on," Xavier said.

"You never really know with that owl." There was a fair chance he was listening to our conversation, but I'd expected him to show his face when he found out the corridor had reappeared. "He'd want to negotiate outrageous terms if we tried to persuade him to unlock the door by carrying the keys in his beak."

"What a visual," he said. "Can familiars be affected by curses too?"

"Yeah, but Sylvester is… not a typical familiar." It had been impossible to keep the owl's true identity a secret from Xavier, and it wasn't as if I didn't tell him everything else. "I can guarantee he's as uncurseable as a Reaper, but he's also stubborn as hell. I could try luring him upstairs with the book-wyrms, but that might not be enough to bribe him into facing an unknown curse."

"More book-wyrms?" he asked. "Never a dull moment, is there?"

"That's how we ended up on this floor." I dropped my

voice. "Since these things tend to come in threes, have you heard anything more about... you know, the Founders?"

"No," he replied. "But that's to be expected. They're lying low."

"After I destroyed their house," I added. "I figured, but I expected them to make a move at some point."

"Their leader's in jail, which is bound to slow them down."

"True, but that didn't stop him from sending me threatening messages." Mortimer Vale wanted me to know he was watching me, that he knew what I was doing. At the thought, the skin on the back of my neck prickled, and my heart gave a lurch when a faint whispering noise sounded behind me, like fabric being dragged across the floor. From behind the door.

I spun to look through the crack in the doorframe, but the lack of light made it impossible to see what had made the noise.

"Rory?" Xavier touched my arm. "What is it?"

"I swear I heard a noise."

"I can look." He darted through the door while I waited for a moment, heart in my throat. I might have wondered if I'd tempted fate by talking about the vampires in the presence of a door that might hide any number of secrets, but Grandma hadn't made an enemy of the vampires as far as I was aware.

Xavier emerged, shaking his head. "Nobody's there."

"I hope you're right." I shivered. "That's what I get for talking about you-know-who."

"I don't blame you for being on edge." He looked up. "Ah—there's your cousin."

Estelle strode towards us, looking frazzled. "That shifter—he's called Walter—is a real pain. This isn't the first time he's been kicked out for eating in the library, but I'm inclined to believe he didn't open the door himself."

"I doubt someone who isn't familiar with the library is responsible for opening the door," I said. "Though now that you mention it—you remember the woman we saw up here before we found the book-wyrms?"

"Oh, her? I saw her downstairs, don't worry," she said distractedly. "I guess she must have taken off when that book started screaming."

"I'm glad we don't have to rescue anyone else," I said. "I swear I heard a noise behind the door just then, though. Xavier looked, but he didn't see anything."

"You did?" she said. "Well, weird noises are par for the course in here. Honestly, I have no idea what Grandma kept in the corridor. The possibilities are literally limitless."

"Yeah, I haven't forgotten that Manifestation Curse," I said, referring to the time when someone had set off a curse that had caused several of Aunt Candace's novels to come to life, with chaotic effects. In fact, the library itself was the product of a similar curse on a larger scale. "Which reminds me… if we can't lock the door, how can we stop anyone with dishonest intentions from getting inside? No spell we put on the stairs to keep people out is going to be a hundred percent foolproof."

"I doubt anyone outside of our family even remembers the missing corridor exists," she said. "Much less expected it to reappear."

True. Maybe I was being paranoid, but the person who'd set off the Manifestation Curse a few months ago had been a former friend of my dad's, and his anger and jealousy had almost destroyed the library. While the library itself was semi-sentient, that didn't mean it couldn't be manipulated… and it didn't mean it couldn't do us any harm.

"I guess we'll have to trade shifts to watch the place until we can figure out a way forward," I said. "Work out a schedule."

"I don't mind staying here," Xavier said. "I don't have any souls to Reap."

"That's always a good thing," said Estelle, "but you don't have to volunteer to stay here all day. Also, I think it's better if a member of the family is here at all times. Just in case it only reacts to us."

"That's what I thought." I reached into my pocket and pulled out the key she'd given me. "The key didn't work for Xavier, either, though it's a pain that none of us can try ourselves."

"Oh." Estelle held out a hand as I passed her the key. "Yeah, I should have guessed. Though if the keys only work for our family members, I'm not sure even Spark or Jet would count."

"What about Sylvester?" I asked. "He's the embodiment of the library itself."

"Yeah, and it's nearly impossible to get him to do anything he doesn't want to," Estelle said. "I can take the first shift and watch the door. Or Cass. I'm surprised she's stayed downstairs as long as she has."

"I forgot we left her in charge of the desk." Though I didn't know that I trusted her to watch the corridor either. "Are you sure we can count on her not to disappear into her room at the first opportunity?"

"See what she thinks of the idea," said Estelle. "Or did you want to take the first shift instead?"

Xavier cleared his throat. "I should probably go. My boss might retract permission for me to take the evening off if he finds out I've spent the afternoon wandering around a cursed corridor."

"He knows you can't be cursed, right?" I headed for the stairs nevertheless, part of me relieved to leave the corridor behind and another part of me wishing I could have gone inside myself.

"Yes, but you know what he's like." He descended the stairs alongside me. "Best to keep him happy."

"Has he ever been happy in his entire undead existence?" Doubtful, but the guy was downright overprotective of his apprentice, especially given that said apprentice was pretty much indestructible. "We're still on for tonight?"

"Sure, if you don't end up in charge of watching the fourth floor."

"Right." Maybe I should have volunteered to take the first watch so I'd be free to go on a date with Xavier that evening. "I'll see what the others think."

When we reached the lower floor and the Reading Corner, Aunt Candace took one look at Xavier and screamed. "It's a Reaper!"

Everyone in the nearby beanbags and hammocks looked in our direction. *Uh-oh.*

"This is Xavier," I said to my aunt. "You won't remember, but he and I are together."

"You've come to Reap my soul?" She scrambled back, almost falling out of her seat. "I won't let you!"

"I'll go," Xavier said hastily. "Really, it's fine. Ah—and I'll refrain from mentioning the corridor to my boss."

"Might not be long before you have no choice." With one eye on my aunt, I followed him out of the Reading Corner and towards the front desk.

Cass looked up with disinterest. "Leaving already? What's she screaming about this time?"

"Xavier." I gave him a brief hug goodbye and a whispered apology before he left the library. "She thinks he came to Reap her soul."

Cass gave a laugh. "I wish I'd seen."

"It wasn't that exciting. Where's your mum?"

"There." She pointed into the stacks, where I found Aunt Adelaide returning a pile of textbooks to the reference section.

"Xavier tried Estelle's key, and it didn't work," I explained to my aunt. "It might only react to a family member."

"I should hope so," she said in absent tones. "Is Candace okay? I heard screaming…"

"She thought Xavier came to take her soul."

"She didn't, did she?" She gave a faint groan. "I should have taken her back to her room, but I didn't think it would do any harm to leave her in the Reading Corner while I checked to make sure none of our recent returns have more unwanted book-wyrms inside them."

"Good thinking." I'd nearly forgotten the book-wyrms in the wake of everything else. "This isn't great timing, but Estelle and I wondered if we should trade shifts watching the corridor. I know it's going to be tricky to work out, since one of us needs to be at the front desk too…"

"We'll manage," she said. "I'll take over the front desk from Cass if she wants to go upstairs first. I'm sure she'll be keen to check up on her animals."

"Estelle's already up there, but I can let her know." I ducked out from behind the shelves and found Cass had returned to reading her book. "Aren't you going to help your mum? I'm sure she'd appreciate another pair of hands."

"I thought you wanted me to stay here." She snapped the book closed. "Or do you want me to take over from Estelle?"

"Only if you promise not to disappear into your animals' room instead."

"Why would that be a bad thing?" She stood, tucking the book under her arm. "I'm sure the corridor isn't going anywhere. As long as one of us is in the general vicinity, it should be fine."

"We can't take any chances, at least until we know what set off the curse."

"What curse?" yawned a voice.

Cass stiffened, while I swivelled to the newcomer—Laney, my best friend. She leaned on the doorway to the living quarters with a vampire's typical languid grace despite being half asleep.

"Aunt Candace is under a spell," I told her. "We found the missing fourth-floor corridor, and it must have erased her memory."

She blinked. "There's a missing corridor?"

"Didn't one of us mention it before?" I looked to my cousin, but Cass said nothing. While her hostility had mostly disappeared after she'd acquired a pendant that would prevent Laney from reading her thoughts, that didn't mean the two of them got along. Not even remotely.

"You might have," said Laney. "I don't remember everything, especially as there isn't a map."

"Yeah, we probably forgot." Laney's transformation into a vampire had led to her getting a crash course in the magical world, and we'd been too busy trying to keep her from getting herself killed by another vampire to share every single one of the library's many quirks.

"It vanished before I was born, and it's not a priority," said Cass, her tone carefully neutral. "Our grandmother's doing, naturally."

"Why'd it show up now?" Her eyes widened. "Oh. Your aunt Candace?"

"That's what we assumed," I said, "but since she doesn't actually remember finding the corridor, we don't know the details. Also, the rest of us can't risk going inside in case we end up getting cursed as well."

She blinked. "Well… I could take a look."

"You could," said Cass. "The curse won't affect vampires, I bet."

Strange. I'd thought she didn't want Laney to get involved in anything that was supposed to be our family's business alone, but she was acting almost... friendly towards her. Which made a change.

"Are you sure?" I directed the question more at Cass than at Laney. "I assume it won't affect vampires, but it's still risky."

"I'm sure," said Laney. "Bring it on."

5

A few minutes later, Cass stood in front of the door to the fourth floor, her hands on her hips. "So this is the corridor that broke Aunt Candace?"

"Not permanently, I hope." I beckoned Laney to come closer. "Estelle used her gloves to open it, but I don't think there's a curse on the door itself."

The door had changed colours to a swampy green at some point since our last trip upstairs. Estelle had agreed to trade places with Cass to watch the desk, though I expected the latter to disappear into her magical monsters' room while Laney and I were occupied.

Laney stepped up behind me, her gaze roving over the wooden surface. "What does a curse generally look like?"

"It doesn't look like anything," said Cass. "It's invisible. Haven't you figured that one out yet?"

"Cass." I gave her a warning look, but despite her hostile words, her attention was focused on the door and not on Laney. "It's usually on an object. Or a place, but that shifter guy wandered in there without being hit by the same curse as our aunt."

Cass stepped forward and nudged the door farther open with her elbow. "The door's fine. If you ask me, it's the corridor itself that has a curse on it."

"That doesn't mean there isn't anything else in there that might be dangerous."

Cass gave a shrug. "I can guarantee I've seen worse."

Hmm. Given the contents of the Magical Creatures Division, she might have had a point there.

"A shifter got in?" asked Laney.

"Yeah. He got himself stuck in a room full of mirrors after he shifted and couldn't find the way out," I explained. "Xavier helped him. Reapers can't be affected by curses, but they also can't use our family's keys to unlock the other doors."

"Let me try." She held out a hand for the key, which Estelle had loaned us again. "I'm ready to go in."

"Go ahead," I said. "But be careful."

Laney glided through the door and disappeared upstairs, her steps almost as silent as a Reaper's. I half expected Cass to follow her given the expression of interest on her face, but she didn't. Cass didn't usually show much of an interest in anything in the library outside of her favourite corridor, but in this case, I didn't blame her for being intrigued. Who wouldn't want to know what was hidden inside a place that had been missing since before she was born?

After a short pause, Laney emerged. "I didn't see anything except a few doors."

"Did you try opening any of them?" I asked.

"One was already open." She held out the key. "The others wouldn't open for me. Sorry."

Cass tutted. "That figures. Typical Grandma, really. She had to get the last word in."

"I thought you didn't know her." Cass was a couple of years younger than me and hadn't been born until after her grandmother had died, I'd thought.

"It's hard not to know her when we're living inside proof of her ridiculous mind twenty-four seven."

"The library," said Laney. "She created this place single-handedly?"

"She did," Cass confirmed. "Didn't leave us an instruction manual, though. This corridor is going to have to be mapped out like my mother initially did with the library: one floor and one door at a time."

"That must have taken forever." I'd also never seen Cass so chatty, let alone in the presence of Laney. My cousin had eventually warmed up to me over time, but I was family. Laney wasn't, and she had the added bonus of being a vampire who was training with Evangeline. Not to mention a target of the Founders... though in fairness, our entire family was probably on their hit list by now.

"There wasn't much up there," Laney said. "I counted less than ten doors, and around a corner, the corridor just... ended. No other stairs or anything. I can draw a map if it helps."

"Worth a shot." I pulled out my notebook and a pen and handed them to her. "Until we can explore the corridor ourselves, this is our best option."

"If you say so," Cass said sceptically, watching as Laney took up the pen and sketched out a scene.

Her fingers moved with typical vampire speed, but the result was a scribble of lines on the page. "I'm not much of an artist."

"Neither am I." In a weird way, it was nice to know that there were some ways in which my best friend hadn't changed from the person she'd been before the vampire bite. "I'll hand this to my aunt and see what she makes of it."

Laney yawned. "I wish I could be more help."

"You were," I said. "We'll just have to figure out the limits of this curse and how to remove it. Once we've dealt with the security measures, we'll be able to explore the corridor for ourselves."

"I doubt Grandma would have made it that easy." Cass closed the door behind Laney with a snap. "That'll stop anyone else wandering in. I'll take the next shift."

I gave her a suspicious look. "You aren't going in there yourself?"

"I don't have a death wish," she said. "No, I get it. We should keep the door within sight of someone in the family at all times so it doesn't pull another disappearing act."

"That's the plan." Part of me was a little sceptical that she wouldn't run off, but she'd done nothing to indicate that she intended to turn her back on the door. Which made a change. "All right. I'll see if I can find Sylvester. Unlike the rest of us, he doesn't need sleep."

As Laney and I headed for the stairs, I didn't speak until I was sure Cass couldn't hear us. "She's weirding me out."

"How so?" Laney asked.

"By being nice to you for a start."

She shrugged. "All she wanted was for me to get out of her head. Now that I can't read her thoughts, she doesn't feel threatened any longer. Makes life easier."

"Still seems weird to me," I said. "And her offering to help guard the corridor too."

"It affects her the same as the rest of you, doesn't it? I bet she's worried for her animals."

"Might be it." She glided downstairs ahead of me, while I followed more slowly. Usually, Laney wouldn't get up for another few hours; vampires were most active at night, and Evangeline kept her busy with lessons most evenings. I was pretty sure the vampires' leader was also soliciting her help to track down the Founders' current location, which was enough of a commitment without adding the mysterious corridor on top of it.

As we reached the ground floor, I scanned the Reading Corner in case Aunt Candace reacted the same to Laney's presence in the library as she had to Xavier. Granted, a vampire wasn't quite the same as a Reaper, and Aunt Candace had a known weakness for them—but there was no telling how her new personality would respond to the idea that there was an undead living in the library.

Aunt Candace was no longer in the Reading Corner. I assumed Aunt Adelaide had successfully convinced her to go back to her room, so while Laney returned to the living quarters, I found Estelle behind the front desk.

"Where's Cass?" she asked. "You didn't leave her guarding the door, did you?"

"She offered," I replied. "I figured she'd have more sense than to put herself and her animals at risk by walking in there herself. If you ask me, though, we need Sylvester. You'd think he'd love the idea of chasing potential trespassers away from the door."

"I know," Estelle said. "I tried calling for him, and my mum left him all the book-wyrms, but he's staying hidden. He must be in one of his stubborn moods."

"He can't know we found the missing corridor," I said. "Though there's one certain way to get his attention."

"You mean the Book of Questions." Her gaze dropped to the desk. "Do you think he's in there? Sylvester?"

"He always is, but that doesn't mean he's actually willing to listen to me." Sylvester might have been less of an owl and more of a powerful and knowledgeable magical being while he was inside the Forbidden Room, but he remained his usual infuriating self. "Using the book would force him to stop ignoring me altogether, at least."

"Hope so." She rummaged behind the desk for the book, while I wondered if the owl had already sneaked into the corridor without any of us knowing. It wouldn't be beyond him—or Cass either. She, as it turned out, had already known Sylvester's true identity, the same as I had.

I hadn't meant to keep it a secret from the rest of my family, but Sylvester had made it quite clear that he didn't want anyone else to know I'd accidentally unmasked him as the embodiment of the library, and he hadn't reacted well when the secret had finally come out either.

Estelle emerged from behind the desk and handed over the large leather-bound book, which had nothing but a giant question mark on the cover. That pretty much summed up Sylvester, really. I took in a deep breath before flipping it open. "I wish to enter the Forbidden Room."

Even though I'd been in the room countless times, it never ceased to give me vertigo when the book flew wide open of its own accord, and I went tumbling head over heels into its pages. I landed sprawling on my back in a blank-walled room that was like being inside a giant cube.

"You again," said Sylvester's voice as I pushed upright. "Have you really run out of any better ways to get my attention? I won't help with your wyrm problem."

"You should know it's not just the wyrms that we're dealing with," I said to him. "We found the missing fourth-floor corridor. I would have thought you'd know, because you know everything, don't you?"

Silence filled the room. Then came a shout like a thunderclap: "You WHAT?"

Covering my ears, I scrambled backwards, but of course, there was nowhere to run. Not until Sylvester let me out. Or threw me out, as the case might be.

"Sylvester." I lowered my hands. "Aunt Candace found the corridor, but it put a curse on her. She can't remember who any of us are."

"You're deceiving me," the owl said. "You can't have found that corridor. Even *I* can't find it."

"You can't?"

Big mistake. Another loud screech echoed around the small space, and I pressed my hands to my ears until it subsided. Someone was in a sensitive mood today, though it was unusual for Sylvester to completely lose track of an entire floor. Yes, it was the only way it made sense for the corridor to have gone missing for decades, but how could the library hide part of itself from him?

I removed my hands from my ears. "Cass is watching the corridor if you want to go up there and see, but we can't go in there without being cursed. As Aunt Candace found out."

"Of course *she's* the one who got herself cursed."

I nodded, relieved he'd returned to a normal tone of voice. "Even Aunt Adelaide couldn't remove the curse, either with her Biblio-Witch magic or with her wand."

"Obviously," he said. "What's the point in a defensive spell that can easily be countered?"

"Is it supposed to affect members of our family, though?" I asked. "Because our Biblio-Witch magic ought to have been able to get rid of it."

"No."

"What do you mean, no?" I frowned at the wall, assuming the owl was watching me no matter which part of the room I faced. "It's not supposed to affect our family?"

"That was implied, you fridge magnet."

"Right." At least his absurd insults proved he wasn't in total shock, but the question of how he'd managed to be unaware of an entire floor of the library remained lodged in my brain. "Was Grandma the only person who knew what was in there?"

"Must you persist in asking inane questions?"

"I don't know what else you expect me to do," I said. "I *would* like to ask the Forbidden Room a question, though. How do we undo the curse on Aunt Candace?"

"I already told you that."

"You didn't." I couldn't believe he didn't know anything at all. No way. "How do we undo the curse?"

"I won't stand for this impertinence!"

"Okay, okay!" I yelped when the room tilted, and I slid upward, falling up the wall and then the ceiling—which opened like a cardboard box, tipping me out.

I toppled head over heels and landed on my back next to the desk. A moment after I hit the carpeted floor, I looked up into Estelle's concerned face.

"No luck?" she asked.

"Nope." I pushed to my feet, breathing hard. "He claims that he didn't know we found the missing corridor and was pretty mad when I told him."

"How is that possible?" said Estelle. "I mean... he *is* the library, isn't he?"

"Apparently not the fourth floor." I picked up the Book of Questions, but I didn't dare open it again.

"Grandma must have somehow made that floor exempt from the Book of Questions," she said. "That's bizarre."

"Tell me about it," I said. "He doesn't know how to take the curse off Aunt Candace, either, for the same reason. Though he also said the corridor's security shouldn't affect our family members."

"There must be a way around it." Her lips pursed. "I guess the old curse-breaker might be able to offer some more ideas. I'll pitch that one to my mother and see what she thinks."

"Yeah, and it depends if you want Mr Bennet to know we found the missing corridor," I replied. "He's not exactly our family's biggest fan."

He didn't know Sylvester's true nature, either, but the grumpy curse-breaker had been at odds with the library since its inception. Who knew—maybe my aunts *had* mentioned the corridor to him at some point.

Estelle blew out a breath. "Did Laney not find anything up there either?"

"Nope. She couldn't open the doors." I fished in my pocket for the key and handed it back to her.

"They must be restricted to our family," she concluded. "Aunt Candace must have opened the first door herself. I'll see if my mum's managed to get any sense out of her yet."

"Good call. I'll watch the desk." I returned the Book of Questions to its usual place and spied my familiar perched on a shelf behind the desk. "Hey, Jet."

"Partner, your aunt seems confused," he said. "She doesn't know who I am!"

"Same with the rest of us." I heaved a sigh. "Jet, can you go up to the third floor and make sure Cass hasn't wandered off to check on the manticore?"

"Yes, partner!"

As he took off, I settled in behind the desk. The library was fairly quiet at this time, and while I waited for Estelle's return, I reached into my bag for my dad's journal. I'd got into the habit of spending my spare moments translating more of the coded journal entries that my father had written in the years after he'd left the library to live in the normal world with my mother and me, but this time, I had another purpose. While my dad hadn't been in the library at the time, he often mentioned his former home—and my grandmother too. I hadn't paid too much attention to those references because I'd been more focused on finding references to the vampires, but I had to wonder if he'd dropped any clues about the missing corridor somewhere between its pages.

I hadn't got very far before Estelle returned. "She's upstairs, fascinated by her own research cave."

"Figures." I lifted my head. "I was wondering if my dad might have mentioned Grandma or the fourth-floor corridor in the journal, but I didn't mark the entries in the week she died."

"Good thinking," she said. "Though I would have thought Grandma would have told my mum everything she told him."

"Told me what?" Aunt Adelaide approached us. "I think my sister will keep herself out of trouble while she's upstairs. She's fascinated by her own notebook collection."

"At least one person's happy," said Estelle. "We wondered if Grandma told Rory's dad about what she hid in the corridor."

"She might have," she acknowledged, "but I don't know that he'd have written it down, even in code."

"I'll have another look later." I closed the journal and returned it to my bag. "Aunt Candace managed to figure it out... wait, does she have her notebook with her?"

Aunt Adelaide's eyes widened. "No. She doesn't."

"I haven't seen her notebook since she was up on the third floor," I recalled. "I don't think she brought it down with her."

It hadn't been inside the corridor, or else Xavier or Laney would have stumbled upon it, but the rest of the third floor had been rearranging itself all day, and the notebook might be anywhere.

"She didn't," said Aunt Adelaide, "but I've not known her to come up with a plan without making notes first."

"Exactly." I lifted my head, eyeing the shadowed area above the third-floor balcony. "If she wrote an account of how she rediscovered the corridor before she fell under the curse, it'll be in her notebook."

Aunt Adelaide volunteered to watch the desk while Estelle and I went upstairs in search of Aunt Candace's missing notebook. We found Cass exactly where I'd left her, for a wonder, and Jet perched on top of a nearby bookshelf.

"Back already?" Cass asked. "Didn't you already send your familiar to spy on me because you didn't trust me to wander off?"

"No, we're here to find Aunt Candace's notebook," I said. "We can't find it anywhere, so I figured she must have left it up here."

"I haven't seen it," she said. "Does it really matter if she can't remember writing anything inside it?"

"I thought she might have written down an account of how she figured out how to find the missing corridor," I explained. "She notes down everything, doesn't she?"

Cass snorted. "Because she has a memory like a leaky sieve, I know. I haven't seen anything, but go ahead and look."

She watched as Estelle and I searched the area around

the door for the missing notebook, but we didn't find so much as a scrap of paper. We continued in a circuit of the floor, checking the alcoves and corners that we'd opened in the task of hunting down the book-wyrms, and we even checked the box in which the surviving wyrms had been ensconced in case one of them had taken the notebook as a snack.

"I hope the biting books didn't eat it," I remarked to Estelle.

"I'm pretty sure Aunt Candace put a protective spell on all her notebooks," she replied. "Weird for it to just vanish, though."

"You don't think the library took it, do you?" I asked, recalling when my dad's journal had gone missing, and I'd found the library had shelved it elsewhere. "For safekeeping?"

"I don't know." She walked ahead of me, passing the door to the fourth-floor corridor again.

"No luck?" Cass jerked her head at the door behind her. "It's not in here, is it?"

"No. Xavier or Laney would have found it," I said. "I don't know where else to look. I already used up my question for the Forbidden Room."

"Did you?" Cass arched a brow at me. "What did you ask?"

"How to remove the curse," I answered. "With no luck, because even Sylvester doesn't know what Grandma put inside that corridor. That's not normal, is it?"

"Not in the slightest," said Cass. "I bet he wasn't happy to find a gap in his knowledge."

"No. He yelled at me and then kicked me out of the room without answering my question," I said. "He's supposed to be the expert on the library, but Grandma must have done something to the corridor to exempt it from his knowledge. Why would she do that?"

"Don't ask me," she said. "As for the notebook, I bet Aunt Candace put it somewhere herself and then forgot."

That didn't seem quite right either, but we'd already searched most of the third floor, so Estelle and I headed for the stairs.

"Maybe she did put it somewhere herself," Estelle said. "We can ask. She might remember the notebook itself even if she doesn't know what she wrote in there."

When we reached the ground floor, she led the way across the lobby to the corridor to our family's living quarters. The living room and kitchen were empty, but a smaller staircase led up to our private rooms. Estelle and I climbed to the top floor, where Aunt Candace's door was ajar—another anomaly, as she generally hated anyone bursting into her room when she was working.

The room itself, which she had dubbed her research cave, was full of shelves packed with newspaper cuttings and other paraphernalia, all covered in a thick layer of dust.

Aunt Candace peered out from behind a shelf, smiling as if she was in heaven. "Isn't this wonderful?"

"Sure." I coughed as she knocked a shelf with her elbow, dislodging another cloud of dust. "Ah—did you bring a notebook up here with you?"

"A notebook?" She gestured at the shelves. "There's no shortage in here. I can find one that hasn't been written in yet."

"No—you had one with you earlier. It's yours." I stepped aside as Estelle entered the room behind me. "Is it in your pocket?"

Aunt Candace reached into the pocket of her cloak and pulled out her Biblio-Witch Inventory. "This one?"

"No, but I'll look after that for you." Estelle held out a hand. "It needs, ah, to be shelved."

Good call. There was no telling what kind of disasters

Aunt Candace might unleash if she started randomly tapping words in her Inventory without realising they contained potent magic.

"Oh, of course." She handed over the book with a vague smile. "It's very confusing in here, isn't it? So many rules."

"Uh-huh." I hadn't a clue what to say to that. It was as if my aunt had been abducted and a stranger left in her place.

"Do you remember seeing a notebook floating behind you when you were up on the third floor?" asked Estelle. "When you came out of the upstairs corridor?"

She shook her head. "No. I don't remember anything except the books—and there are a *lot* of them, aren't there? Do you really run this place all by yourselves?"

"Yes," said Estelle, "but this room's yours."

"All mine?" Her vague smile returned, and I backed towards the door, mildly creeped out. "Astonishing."

"Yeah. That's one word for it." I left the room, hearing her exclaiming at the ingenuity of the person who'd set up the research cave as Estelle closed the door behind her.

"I'll put this somewhere safe." She held up the Biblio-Witch Inventory. "Until we get that curse off her."

"Wise idea." I led the way downstairs, where we returned to the lobby.

At the front desk, we found Aunt Adelaide flipping through the Book of Questions and muttering to herself. "Really, Sylvester."

"He wouldn't let you in?" I guessed.

"No, he wouldn't." She closed the book. "You didn't find the notebook?"

"No, and it wasn't in her pockets either," I said. "I thought the library might have shelved it, like that time with the journal."

"It's possible, but it's more likely to want to shelve this." Estelle held up the Biblio-Witch Inventory she'd taken from our aunt. "I'll put it in one of the top-security rooms. Is that okay, Mum?"

"Of course. Good thinking." She shook her head at the Book of Questions. "I assume a certain owl is feeling insulted at being left out of my mother's plans."

"That's the impression I got from him," I said. "He might get over his sulk if we give him enough time, but I wonder if *he* knows where the notebook is."

"Inside the corridor?" Aunt Adelaide suggested.

"Xavier and Laney didn't find it," I said, "but if the corridor is capable of moving things around the way the rest of the library is..."

"Then the corridor might have hidden the notebook to prevent the information on how to access it from being shared?" Estelle suggested. "Is it possible for a security spell to be that sophisticated?"

"That would depend on the spell," said Aunt Adelaide. "My mother's spells were never entirely predictable."

"I guess Aunt Candace had to get it from somewhere," I said. "I mean, another theory is that the book-wyrms or the books with teeth ate the notebook while she was distracted."

"Unlikely," she said. "After the incident with her manuscript, I'd be surprised if she didn't put a spell on her notebook to prevent it from being damaged."

"We could try a summoning spell?" Estelle suggested, pulling out her own Biblio-Witch Inventory. "It might not work if the notebook turns out to be in the corridor, but otherwise, it should be able to reach any corner of the library."

"Worth a shot." As I watched, she ran her finger down the page and tapped the word *summon*. My skin tingled with static, but no notebook appeared.

"Let's see." Aunt Adelaide pulled out her own Biblio-Witch Inventory, and I moved to do the same. "*Summon.*"

I tapped the word with my own fingertip, but even when the three of us cast the spell at the same time, the notebook didn't reappear.

"Is it in the corridor?" I thought back to the noise I thought I'd heard, and a shiver ran down my spine. "It's out of reach of our magic…"

"That or it was somehow removed from the library." Estelle put her Biblio-Witch Inventory away. "Which shouldn't be possible."

"Maybe that shifter stole it," I suggested. "What did you say his name was, Walter?"

"Nah, he can't have taken the notebook," Estelle said. "He only had his clothes because Xavier found them in the corridor."

"What about the other woman?" I racked my mind for ideas. "The one in the hammock. Is she still in here?"

"Who?" asked Aunt Adelaide.

"A witch," I said. "She was up on the third floor at the same time as the shifter, but Estelle thought she went downstairs before the door to the fourth-floor corridor appeared."

"I can look for her," Estelle offered. "I wanted to make sure she wasn't cursed, but I was only half paying attention at the time."

"All right." This was a long shot, but if there'd only been two people up on the third floor at the time and one of them was already accounted for, it was worth checking up on the other to see if she'd noticed anything when the fourth-floor corridor had appeared. Including Aunt Candace's notebook.

"Which book of Aunt Candace's was she reading again?" I asked Estelle as we walked through the towering stacks towards the Reading Corner. "I didn't see."

"A romance one." She scanned the beanbags and hammocks tucked between the shelves. "No… she's not here. Must have gone home."

"Did she take the book with her?" I turned away, and we retraced our steps to the front desk. There, Aunt Adelaide had put away the Book of Questions and was flipping through the record book instead.

"Can I have a look in there?" asked Estelle.

"Of course." Her mother stood back to let her turn to the most recent page. "This witch might be a witness, do you think?"

Estelle studied the page. "Weird. Someone checked out five of Aunt Candace's books at once—but from five of her different pen names."

"Someone knows all her alter egos?" I frowned. "How many people are aware of every one of Aunt Candace's pen names?"

"Not many people," Aunt Adelaide said. "Most of the locals know one or two, but even after the incident last year, people are surprisingly unobservant. Who is it?"

"Lisa Grubbins," Estelle said. "Was she the witch we saw upstairs, I wonder? She was reading one of Aunt Candace's romance novels…"

"A fan, is she?" Aunt Adelaide's mouth turned down at the corners. "The name rings a bell…"

"I can ask Cass," I offered. "She must have been the one who checked out the books."

"True," Estelle said. "But Cass isn't known for paying attention when she's dealing with the public."

"You never know." I was more inclined to think the notebook was inside the corridor somewhere that Xavier and Laney hadn't had access to.

If one of us stood on the threshold and used a summoning spell, might *that* work? It was worth a try, so I headed back to the stairs and climbed up to the third floor alone.

Cass rolled her eyes when she saw me. "If you want to trade places, just ask."

"I'm not here to trade places," I said. "Did you help a woman check out five of Aunt Candace's books from the library earlier?"

She blinked. "Why?"

"I wondered if it was the same woman who I saw up here." I paced over to the hammock where I'd seen the witch, but the stack of books she'd been reading was no longer there. The notebook wasn't there either, but that was to be expected.

"What woman?" Cass asked when I returned to the door. It'd changed colours again, to a deep blue, which made me wonder if it was cycling through all the colours of the rainbow.

"She was in the hammock over there." I pointed over my shoulder. "Near the shifter we found up in the corridor."

"You think she might have sneaked in too?"

"I don't know, but she was reading one of Aunt Candace's books… did you open the door?"

The door had opened a little behind Cass, revealing a crack of shadow. "No, I didn't."

I peered behind her. "It didn't open itself, did it?"

"Don't be ridiculous." She didn't budge, though her shoulders tensed. "Must have been a draught."

"You don't really think that, do you?" A chill sprang to my arms. "Is there anyone in there?"

"You're cracking up," she said. "Nobody's here."

"We're in a magical library," I pointed out. "With a vampire in the basement, among other things. If there *is* someone living in there, it's not the least likely explanation."

"If you saw or heard someone, I would have heard them too," she retaliated.

There is that. We had better things to do than argue, and

for all I knew, she was right, and I was imagining things. "I wondered if Aunt Candace's notebook might have gone missing in there. None of our summoning spells worked."

"Which means it's out of the scope of the library," she surmised. "You think the corridor hid it somewhere? Why?"

"To prevent anyone else from learning how to access the corridor."

She raised a brow. "Bit late for that now."

"I don't know where else it could be," I said. "Unless… do you remember who checked out all those books? She picked up five books from five of Aunt Candace's different pen names, which takes dedication."

She grunted. "If she's a witness, feel free to track her down, but all I did was check out her books. I don't remember anything else about her."

"Okay." My gaze drifted to the shadowy gap in the door again. "Maybe keep that closed if you can."

"Noted." Her face showed no fear or surprise. That was Cass for you, though—completely unflappable even in the face of a door that seemed to have mysteriously opened by itself.

Maybe I am cracking up. Shaking off the sense of unease, I returned to the ground floor. There, Aunt Adelaide remained behind the desk, but Estelle had disappeared.

"Hey," I said to my aunt. "Cass doesn't remember anything odd about the witch who checked out the books. Where's Estelle?"

"She's gone to research Lisa Grubbins." A concerned look flitted over her face. "I'm pretty sure someone with that name was once on my sister's list of mortal enemies."

"She has a list of mortal enemies?" That was typical of Aunt Candace, really, but in her current state, I doubted she remembered who any of those enemies were. "Then why would this woman be reading five of her books at once?"

"Exactly what I'd like to know." She swivelled towards the living quarters, from which a thudding noise sounded. "I think my sister has come downstairs."

"Oh boy." I veered that way and found Aunt Candace clattering around the kitchen, humming cheerfully under her breath.

"Hello," she said vaguely. "Where is the coffee maker?"

"Right there." I pointed. "You want to make some coffee?"

Estelle came into the room behind me. "I can help you make it if you like."

"At least that hasn't changed," I said to my cousin in an undertone. "Though it's a bit later in the day than usual."

"What's later in the day?" Aunt Candace asked.

"You normally need coffee to wake up," I explained. "Ah— do you recognise the name Lisa Grubbins?"

"Should I?" She turned on the coffee maker—at least *that* was one skill she hadn't forgotten—and resumed humming under her breath.

"We're trying to figure out who cursed you." That and Lisa had been right next to Aunt Candace before she'd lost her memories… and her notebook. "Right, Estelle?"

"Right." Estelle watched for a moment as if to gauge that we were safe to leave Aunt Candace to make her own coffee and then beckoned me aside. "Rory—Lisa Grubbins is on her list of enemies as a bully from her school days."

"That's not good." Had this Lisa person maintained a grudge ever since? It was hard to imagine she'd opened the door to the missing corridor, though. "Do you think it's worth talking to her?"

"Given that she has a pile of our books, yes," she said. "Did Cass remember her?"

"Yes, but she wasn't paying close attention when she helped her check out the books." I tried to ignore Aunt Candace's cheerful humming in the background as we left the kitchen. "The door, though… I swear it opened by itself. Cass said she didn't touch it."

She blinked. "You think there's someone in there?"

"I don't know what to think," I admitted. "This Lisa Grubbins, though… it's weird that Aunt Candace didn't notice she was upstairs. You'd think someone on her list of mortal enemies would have caught her attention."

"Oh, she wasn't paying any attention at all," Estelle commented. "She was even more erratic than usual, and Lisa was lying in a hammock at the time, so we couldn't see her face."

True. We returned to the front desk, where Aunt Adelaide didn't look surprised to learn that Lisa Grubbins occupied a prominent spot on her sister's list of enemies.

"It's worth paying her a visit," Aunt Adelaide said, "but be careful."

"We can start by asking if she saw anything upstairs," Estelle said. "Do you have her address?"

"Yes, it's 14 Lowell Avenue," Aunt Adelaide said. "Rory, you go too, just in case."

I glanced over at the living quarters. "Will Aunt Candace be okay by herself?"

"Yes, there's enough in that research cave of hers to keep her entertained," she replied. "Though I can't imagine her future self will be thrilled if she makes a mess of her own records."

"She'll have to deal with it." We didn't have long before the library closed for the day, and this Lisa Grubbins might be our only remaining witness to Aunt Candace being cursed. Putting that together with their unpleasant history, I couldn't ignore the connection.

Estelle and I crossed the square, which was relatively quiet at this hour, in the lull before people started walking home from work. A cool breeze drifted from the coast;

summer was definitely on its way out, and autumn would soon follow.

"Do you think I'm weird for thinking there might be someone else in that corridor?" I asked Estelle. "Cass denied opening the door, and I'm inclined to believe her."

"No, I don't think you're weird," she said. "There's no telling what our grandmother hid in there. If it were practical, I'd close the whole library to the public until we figure out if it's likely to be a danger."

"The whole library?" True, it was only a matter of time before the other patrons started asking questions about why they weren't allowed up to the third floor, and the corridor was even more of a hazard than the book-wyrms were. "For how long? Until we get the curse off Aunt Candace?"

"That's the problem," she said. "We don't know how long it'll take to uncurse her, and we don't need to draw unnecessary attention. Especially when we might be being watched."

"By… the Founders." I dropped my voice. "Yeah. If they're watching us, it'd be just like them to take advantage of our distraction."

They'd been quiet the past couple of weeks… too quiet, in fact. If not for the unlikeliness of any connection between them and the corridor, I'd wonder if they'd diverted our attention on purpose while they recovered from the blow of losing their hideout.

"I don't think we have to worry about them just yet," Estelle added. "It's the curse that concerns me. I wondered about asking the curse-breaker, but to break a curse, you usually have to find the source. Or the caster."

"We do know the source," I said. "The corridor itself. Though… can you break a curse on something that big?"

"It's not the size that's the issue; it's the fact that it's part of the library."

"Not enough to be part of Sylvester's sphere of knowledge, though." I buried my hands in my pockets as another gust of wind brought the salty tang of the sea air. "As for the caster—well, that's Grandma, isn't it?"

"Yes, which is why we know the curse was cast upon an object or place," she said. "She meant for the curse to outlive her."

"Without leaving instructions as to how to undo it." I walked with Estelle up the high street and then into a cul-de-sac. "If this Lisa Grubbins is on Aunt Candace's list of enemies, why haven't we run into her before?"

"That might explain it." She pointed to a house with a "sold" sign leaning against a sagging garden wall. "A lot of people move away from town for a few years and then come back later."

She must have lived here before if she and Aunt Candace had gone to school together, but the dilapidated state of the house and its overgrown garden suggested nobody had taken care of it for a while.

Estelle rang the doorbell. There was a long pause before the door opened, revealing a middle-aged witch with dyed-blond hair and magenta-painted nails. "What?"

"We're from the library," Estelle said. "Are you Lisa Grubbins?"

"What do you think?" Lisa growled with decided unfriendliness. "What d'you want?"

"You were in the library just then," Estelle said. "Ah—I wondered if you saw our aunt Candace."

The witch's jaw twitched. "Why's that?"

"My mother said you're acquainted," added Estelle. "We're looking for—"

"She and I went to school together," Lisa interrupted. "She killed me off in a book."

Uh-oh. Maybe we should have come up with a cover story for our visit beforehand.

"She does that," I said, thinking hard. "I know she can be a little, er, temperamental and difficult to get along with—"

"Who is it?" called a gravelly voice from behind her.

"Someone from the library, Jamie," she returned. "I'm getting rid of them."

A man with a long, narrow face shuffled into view behind her. I'd have taken him for a weasel shifter if not for the wand he gripped in his hand. A glare slid onto his face when he saw Estelle and me. "You're from that library, are you? Trying to scam us with late fees?"

"Not at all," Estelle said. "I was just talking to your... wife?"

"Fiancée," he growled.

"Fiancée," she repeated. "She checked some books out of the library earlier, and we wanted to, erm..."

"Check for book-wyrms," I blurted. "There was an infestation on the third floor."

I was proud of myself for coming up with that one, but both Jamie and Lisa scoffed.

"A likely story," said Lisa. "You just want to nose around."

"No, it's true," said Estelle. "Book-wyrms feed on paper, and we wanted to make sure they hadn't got into any of the books you checked out. My sister didn't realise how serious the problem was."

"Problem." Jamie snorted. "Sounds like your library has a lot of those."

What would give him that idea? Evidently, Lisa had been bad-mouthing us behind our backs, but it seemed my aunt hadn't put her on her enemy list for nothing. And the feeling was evidently mutual.

"Not at all," I said. "However, I'd appreciate it if we could check the books you brought home. You don't want book-wyrms in your house, do you?"

"S'pose not." Lisa moved aside to let us in. "Fine, but be quick about it."

The dingy hallway smelled of mould, and Jamie gave us an ugly look as he slunk past us into the living room. There, Lisa pointed to a stack of books on a coffee table covered in empty beer cans and takeout containers. "Get on with it."

Estelle picked her way around the cardboard boxes occupying the rest of the floor space while I surreptitiously scanned the room. The only piece of furniture was a leather sofa, and a distinct scratching noise came from somewhere beneath it. I approached warily, my gaze snagging on the edge of a page poking out from underneath the sofa.

"What's that noise?" I nudged the sofa with my knee, and the scratching intensified. It sounded… well, like a pen scribbling on a page.

"Hey!" Jamie shouted in indignation as I nudged the sofa again, freeing the pen that had been trapped beneath it. The pen drifted out and rose into the air, and both Jamie and Lisa exclaimed in outrage when I gave the sofa another nudge to reveal a notebook, similarly pinned down.

"Where'd you get that?" I reached for the notebook, but Jamie stepped into my way before I could yank it free.

"Get out." Jamie pointed his wand in my face. "Stop nosing around my house."

"That's my aunt's pen and notebook." My heart thudded in my chest, his wand inches from my nose. "She enchanted them herself. Why do you have them?"

"None of your business," Lisa said in a shrill voice; she couldn't deny the theft when the pen and notebook were right in front of my face.

Estelle reached behind me and snatched up the pen and notebook, her own wand in her hand. "Those are the property of the library."

"Thieves!" Jamie spun around and cast a spell, which hit

the wall behind Estelle and left a sizzling hole in the wallpaper.

Estelle and I bolted for the door. Another spell hit the wall as we made our way out of the house, and we didn't stop running until we reached the end of the cul-de-sac.

"Now I know why my mum thought I'd need backup," Estelle puffed out as we jogged down the high street. "And I get why that Lisa is on Aunt Candace's mortal enemies list too."

"Agreed," I said breathlessly. "Better hope she *didn't* go into that corridor. She'd never admit to it."

She evidently wasn't cursed, but she'd stolen my aunt's property. If Aunt Candace ever revised her mortal enemies list, Lisa Grubbins and her fiancé would shoot straight to the top.

7

Aunt Adelaide stared at our flushed faces when Estelle and I burst into the library. "What happened?"

"We had to steal back Aunt Candace's pen and notebook." I placed them on the desk, from which they promptly rose into the air again. "I don't know if Lisa Grubbins actually went into the corridor, but she's awful, and her fiancé is almost as bad."

Aunt Adelaide's brows rose. "It's safe to say she didn't trespass in there if her memories are intact."

"More's the pity." Estelle reached for Aunt Candace's notebook and began flipping through it. "I wouldn't be surprised if she *was* involved in our aunt getting cursed, but I have a feeling she won't be returning the books she borrowed in good condition."

"Right. I should have grabbed them too." I peered over her shoulder at Aunt Candace's notebook. "What's it say?"

"Gibberish, mostly," she said. "Notes for her latest book."

"Nothing about the corridor?"

She turned the page. "I'll see. It's possible that Lisa just wanted to swipe her manuscript instead, but she uses a computer for the actual writing. These are just notes."

I watched the pen hover above the desk for a moment. "How does the enchantment on that thing work? I mean, it can't read her thoughts, can it?"

"No," Aunt Adelaide replied. "Sometimes, she dictates to the pen or just tells it to take notes. It's a complex enchantment, and she's trained it to mimic her writing style. In fact, Lisa might have stolen it for that reason alone."

"But she didn't make any notes on the missing corridor?" She must have, surely.

"I'll check," Estelle said, flipping over a page. "If I can decipher her handwriting."

"And I thought my dad's journal was hard to read." My own handwriting was by no means perfect, but Aunt Candace's looked as if a parrot had got hold of a fountain pen in its beak and scribbled all over the page. I could make out a few words if I squinted, but "corridor" wasn't one of them, and neither was "fourth floor."

"I know, right?" She continued to flip through the pages, but it swiftly transpired that they consisted mostly of random notes and observations, not instructions on how to find a missing corridor.

"Weird," I commented. "I wonder if she was using a different notebook?"

Had we made enemies of Lisa and her fiancé for no reason? In fairness, it was better than Aunt Candace marching over to their house herself to find the stolen notebook and pen, but in her current state, she had no memory of their rivalry.

"If she was, there are dozens up in her research cave," said Estelle. "It'll take hours to search—"

There came an alarming roar from elsewhere in the library, and both of us jumped violently. "What *was* that?"

Estelle paled. "I think that might have been Cass's manticore."

"I'll look." I ran for the stairs, my heart racing. While there weren't many patrons left in the library in the hour before we closed for the night, we didn't need another crisis on our hands.

Several crashes greeted my arrival at the third floor, and I followed the noise to the open door to Cass's favourite corridor. Inside, I found Cass attempting to push a large animal with a scorpion's tail and a furred, lionlike head back into its cage.

"Need a hand?"

"No," she grunted, shoving the beast's flank. "Calm *down*."

"Are you sure you should be shoving a manticore?" I reached for my wand. "I don't think that's going to help calm it down—"

The beast's teeth snapped at the air, narrowly missing Cass's shoulder, as she finally heaved its huge body over the threshold of the cage. "There."

Her wand flicked, and the cage door clicked shut. I raised my own wand when the beast lunged forward, rattling the cage bars, but Cass stepped in my way. "Don't you even think about casting a spell on him."

"I'm trying to stop him from eating your face, Cass."

Behind her, the manticore growled, as if to underscore my words.

"He's not going to hurt me," she said. "*You*, on the other hand, might not be so lucky."

Taking the hint, I backed out of the room. "How'd he escape? Was the cage unlocked?"

"No," Cass answered. "You don't think I'd let him out on purpose, do you?"

No. For a wonder. Frowning, I walked out of Cass's corridor and turned left, heading for the door to the fourth-floor corridor.

The door stood slightly ajar, as if someone had opened it to take a peek. *Cass... or someone else?* I hesitated for an instant then reached into my pocket for my gloves. As I was pulling them on, a faint noise sounded behind me, like fabric scraping across the ground. Movement stirred in the corner of my eye.

I spun on my heel. "Cass?"

No answer. I could have sworn the movement had resembled a person stepping out of sight behind a shelf, but my cousin didn't answer me. Heart in my throat, I trod across the carpeted floor, but when I peered around the shelf, there was nobody to be seen.

"Cass?" I returned to the open door to the fourth-floor corridor and pushed it closed with gloved hands. "Was that you?"

"What?" She came marching over, from the opposite direction from where I'd seen the movement. "Did you just close the door?"

"Yes—is there someone else up here?" I pointed towards the spot where I thought I'd seen the figure. "I swear I saw something moving over there."

"Are you sure one of those books isn't on the loose again?"

"I forgot about those." Had one of them opened the manticore's cage? They didn't have hands, but some had claws, and they were certainly mobile enough. *Weird, though.*

Cass shrugged and retook her position in front of the fourth-floor corridor. "That's sorted. Unless you want to take the next shift?"

"No—I mean, I can, but Estelle and I found Aunt

Candace's notebook," I told her. "We can't find any mention of the corridor."

"You found it?" she asked. "Was it in her pocket?"

"No, Lisa Grubbins stole it," I said. "You know the witch who was up here earlier? Turns out she seized on the chance to swipe Aunt Candace's notes. Seems she's on her list of mortal enemies."

Her brows shot up. "I'm surprised she isn't banned from the library."

"You know her?" I blinked. "Cass, you're the one who helped her check out five books. Did you know she used to bully Aunt Candace at school?"

"No, but anyone who's on Aunt Candace's list of mortal enemies should be banned from the library for their own safety."

"Ha." She wasn't wrong. "Seriously, though. Lisa and her fiancé are both nasty pieces of work, but so far, the notebook hasn't revealed any proof she knew what was going on up here."

"Who, Lisa Grubbins or Aunt Candace?"

"Both." Unbidden, my eyes went to the door again; it was more of a violet colour than the blue it'd been earlier. "If Aunt Candace made notes in a different notebook, it'll be hard to find out which. She has a hundred or more note-books in her research cave and can't remember what any of them are for."

"Good luck with that," she said. "You know, on second thought, I'd rather stay here instead. I'll make sure nobody else messes around with my animals."

"All right. I'll see you later." I headed for the stairs, wondering if Cass was nearly as sceptical as she pretended to be. It was hard to deny that her manticore escaping its cage while nobody else was on the third floor was a cause for concern. While it was entirely possible that we'd missed picking up one of the runaway books, that didn't strike me as likely.

Downstairs, I found Estelle continuing to flip through the notebook. "The manticore got out?"

"Yeah, but I don't know how," I said. "Someone unlocked the cage, but the only person up there is Cass."

"Are you sure it wasn't her?"

"No, she wouldn't scare her own pet on purpose."

"You'd be surprised at some of the things she's done for attention," she said. "But no, I guess not. She might have left it unlocked by accident instead, though."

I glimpsed movement in the living quarters and saw Aunt Adelaide descending the stairs, leading Aunt Candace behind her. "What's your mum doing?"

"I think she's going to fetch the curse-breaker," she said in an undertone. "To ask him to look at Aunt Candace."

"Rory?" Leaving her sister, Aunt Adelaide walked over to the front desk. "What happened up there?"

"The manticore escaped," I explained. "Cass said she didn't leave the cage door unlocked, so I'm not sure how it got out."

"Concerning." Her expression clouded. "I'd have a look up there, but we don't have long before the curse-breaker's shop closes for the night, and I wanted him to look at Candace."

"Good call." My gaze travelled to the living room, where Aunt Candace sat on the sofa, wearing her uncustomary blank-faced expression. "We didn't find anything in the notebook either, right, Estelle?"

"Nope," said Estelle. "Not for lack of trying. Do you want me to help you take Aunt Candace to see Mr Bennet?"

"No—I don't think it's a good idea to take her out of the library." She lowered her voice. "She doesn't know the town, and I'm concerned she might wander off and get into trouble."

"Are you sure he'll agree to come here?" Estelle asked. "I suppose he might want to look at her for the novelty alone."

"I'll make it worth his while." Aunt Adelaide strode towards the door, her navy cloak billowing behind her. "Make sure she doesn't get into mischief, won't you?"

"I'll try," said Estelle. "Hopefully, there won't be any more incidents upstairs..."

"Don't jinx it." It was lucky the manticore hadn't made it down from the third floor and that nobody else had been up there at the time. "Cass wondered if one of the books was still wandering around and unlocked the door."

"Seems a bit too intelligent for a book, even one from the Magical Creatures Division." Estelle watched the door close behind her mother. "I don't know what else could have done it, though."

"Begone!" shouted Aunt Candace.

Uh-oh. I swivelled in her direction, but I couldn't see who she was shouting at. "Aunt Candace?"

"Get away from me!"

Alarmed, I ran towards her shout, followed by Estelle. We reached the living room, where Aunt Candace stood on the sofa, pointing at a small figure hovering in the air.

"That's just Spark." Estelle beckoned, and the pixie flew behind her, its little wings beating anxiously. "He works here."

Aunt Candace huffed, but she climbed down off the sofa. "This place is playing tricks on me. Glitter and shadows."

"It's just the library," said Estelle. "I have to watch the desk —Rory?"

"Come on, Aunt Candace." I beckoned her into the kitchen. "I can make you a hot chocolate. Or another coffee." Not that she needed the caffeine, really.

"I won't be bribed," she said. "You're the lost cousin, are you? My sister told me about you."

"I'm not lost. But yes, I get called that sometimes." I might have found her wide-eyed innocence endearing if it hadn't been so *weird.* "If you sit down, I can bring you something to read. What do you like?"

"Hmm?" She stared vacantly into space. "I don't remember."

"Well, we have pretty much everything." I scanned the living room and spotted a stack of books sitting on the table. "Pick what you like. Or something from upstairs."

She strode towards the stairs. "I think I shall have another look at those notebooks."

"Well… all right." I watched her leave the room and climb the stairs, hoping that we'd be able to bring her back down later when Mr Bennet arrived. She certainly wouldn't want him going into her research cave—though it was anyone's guess as to how much of this she'd remember afterwards.

I returned to the front desk to wait for Aunt Adelaide to return with the curse-breaker in tow.

When she did, the sour-faced old man glared at the library when he walked in as if it had personally insulted him by existing—which was understandable enough given that my aunts had once asked him to undo the spell that had created the library and had then changed their minds.

"Your sister's got herself cursed, has she?" he said to Aunt Adelaide. "Are you sure you want her to get her memories back? I imagine she's much easier to manage without them."

"I'd prefer for her to be back to normal," Aunt Adelaide replied. "Especially as the curse isn't supposed to affect members of our family."

"But you're fine with setting it loose on the public?" He eyed the handful of patrons who remained in the Reading Corner. "Have you told them?"

"It's not loose in here," I told him. "Aunt Candace went into a specific place she shouldn't have."

"The fourth-floor corridor," said Aunt Adelaide. "You know the one."

His mouth opened in surprise. *He knows, then.* I was surprised she'd readily told him if he hadn't already known, but if she wanted him to undo the curse, it was wise to let him know what he was in for. "You found it, did you?"

"Candace did," she answered. "We assume she walked into a security spell put on the corridor by its creator."

"Ah." He jerked his head towards the living quarters. "Is she in there?"

"She's in her room," I explained. "She got herself frightened by the pixie, and I suggested she find something to read."

"I'll bring her downstairs." Aunt Adelaide strode towards the living quarters, while Estelle and I waited by the desk with the old curse-breaker.

Mr Bennet was the first to break the awkward silence. "The rest of you aren't cursed?"

"Not as far as we're aware," I replied. "Cass is watching the door to make sure it doesn't disappear again."

He snorted. "I'd ask if that's likely, but in this place, you'll be lucky if that's all it does. You really have no plans to tell the public?"

"We don't currently have any intention to make an announcement," Estelle said. "Mostly because we don't know *what* to warn them about. We already intend to bar everyone from the third floor, but that's because we had a book-wyrm outbreak earlier."

The curse-breaker shook his head. "It's no wonder people call this place a hazard. I had someone at my shop less than an hour ago saying the same thing."

"Not Lisa Grubbins?" I asked.

"I don't know that name," he said. "It was a man. A wizard. Said you cursed his fiancée."

"What?" I frowned. "That's nonsense. His fiancée stole Aunt Candace's notebook. He tried to curse *us* when we took it back."

Estelle blew out a breath. "If he's spreading lies about us—"

"There she is." Mr Bennet went over to the living room, where Aunt Adelaide had returned with Aunt Candace.

"Who are you?" she asked him. "A doctor?"

"You really are cursed, aren't you?" Mr Bennet tutted. "Right, I'll see what I can do."

As he moved towards the living quarters, the front door opened, and a group of students came into the library. Typically, they'd decided to come in at the last minute, wanting a stack of complicated textbooks, and Estelle and I were kept busy while Mr Bennet examined Aunt Candace. It wasn't until after the students had departed the library that Mr Bennet finally walked out of the living room.

"What's the verdict?" I asked. "Did you manage to undo the curse?"

"No, but I didn't expect to," he said. "Unless you can bring me the object that cursed her or else convince the person responsible to undo it."

"That's impossible," Estelle protested. "The curse was cast on a corridor, and none of us can go in there without ending up in the same state. Also, the person responsible—our grandmother—has been dead since the year I was born."

"Then there's nothing more I can do," he replied. "The person responsible created the library, and that's where you should look for your solution."

The library is semi-sentient. Was the library involved in the curse? No, even Sylvester hadn't been able to undo it. The fourth floor was another entity altogether.

As the curse-breaker made to leave, I asked, "Is there at least a way to stop the rest of us from getting hit by the same curse?"

"No," he said. "Curses are the most powerful type of magic there is. There's no blocking one, especially one as powerful as the curse on your aunt."

"There must be something, though," I said desperately. "If it's not going to wear off, and the only means of undoing it is in the same corridor none of us can go into…"

"Candace should have thought of that before she opened the door." He turned away. "Try not to get any members of the public cursed, won't you?"

As he left the library, my shoulders slumped. "His attitude hasn't improved, has it?"

"It's concerning that he can't fix her, but it was a long shot," said Estelle. "I wonder if the solution *is* in the corridor. Hidden away."

"I guess we can ask Xavier and Laney to look for it, but if neither of them can open any of the doors…"

"One of us will think of something, I'm sure," said Estelle. "Oh, and we should come up with a shift schedule for watching the door."

"Cass wanted to stay up there for now, but I can take the next watch," I offered. "Wait, I was meant to go on a date with Xavier, but I can bring him here and send him on another expedition into the corridor."

"That's hardly a substitute for a date."

"It's no big deal," I said. "Laney will be at a vampire lesson and won't be able to look around this evening. Xavier won't mind helping us."

"I guess," she said. "All right. You take the evening shift, and I'll take the night one. Mum can take over from me in the morning."

"Assuming she isn't still watching Aunt Candace," I added.

"We should keep an eye out for Lisa Grubbins too. She strikes me as petty enough to come back for revenge when we're not looking."

"Yeah, and her fiancé." Her lips pursed. "We haven't seen the last of them, I'm betting."

8

Xavier showed up later that evening to pick me up for our date, and I gave him the news.

"I've volunteered to take the evening shift upstairs, but we can grab a takeaway from somewhere and have a picnic up there," I told him. "If that's okay with you, that is."

"Of course," he said. "If you had to choose between that and the night shift, I don't blame you for picking the evening."

"I also thought you could have another look around if you wanted to," I added. "Laney is at a vampire lesson, and none of the rest of us can take the risk of going in there."

We ordered fish and chips and took them up to the third floor. With the warm light cast by the floating lanterns onto the shelves, it was actually a pretty nice place for a picnic if you ignored the ominous presence of the closed door and the knowledge that there was an angry manticore not far away. Not to mention the man-eating books.

"It's quiet," Xavier remarked. "I thought you said Cass's manticore was in a temper."

"Guess he's calmed down," I commented. "It was weird. She said she didn't unlock the cage, and I don't think she'd accidentally leave it open either."

"It's not surprising that this floor is a little unbalanced after the book-wyrm incident," he said. "Haven't things been moving around all day?"

"True." I wiped grease off my fingers onto a napkin. "Maybe I'm paranoid. Cass thinks so, but I… I didn't like the idea of being up here alone."

"Understandable." He watched me for a moment, the lanterns' reflection flickering in his aquamarine eyes. "If it helps, there's nothing up here that triggers my Reaper senses in any way."

"Nothing dead, you mean?" I relaxed a little. "Actually, that does help. Though Grandma's ghost is probably the least threatening thing that might come out of the corridor."

There was no good reason for her ghost to have stuck around without contacting any of my family members, though, right?

When we'd finished eating, Xavier offered to explore the corridor again. "Want me to test out those keys?"

"Sure thing." I reached over and handed him the bundle of keys Estelle had given me. Then, to take my mind off the door, I flipped my dad's journal open on my lap.

"Making progress?" asked Xavier.

"Not exactly—I was actually looking for references to my grandmother," I explained. "Dad had already left the magical world behind at that point, but it's not like he never thought about the library. I wondered if he'd dropped any clues about what she hid in the corridor."

"It's worth checking," Xavier agreed. "I'll be right back."

Silently, he vanished behind the door, while I suppressed an inexplicable impulse to follow him. I hadn't been kidding when I'd said I didn't want to be up here alone, but the idea of *him* going upstairs on his own in the darkness made me uneasy too. No spell or curse could outdo a Reaper, but the weight of my family's secrets seemed starker with the journal in front of me. It was a reminder that some would kill for that knowledge.

I didn't know if Grandma's secrets were as intense as Dad's, but his had unintentionally caused my first introduction to the magical world when a group of knowledge-hunting vampires had tried to intimidate me into handing over the journal. While I'd come to understand how he'd made enemies of the Founders, the journal so far contained no references to the corridor, and he only mentioned the library itself in passing.

Regardless, it was plain from what I'd read that he'd missed the world he'd left behind, along with the rest of his family members. He'd started the journal the year I was born, so I flipped back to the start to find the entries around the time of Grandma's death. Pity one couldn't do the magical equivalent of a Google search on a physical book... or if you could, it wasn't a spell I knew yet.

After a minute of searching, I did find a reference to the day of Grandma's funeral, but he'd only written a short entry for that day, and I hadn't paid much attention the first time I'd read it. The entry read, *Mum's funeral was today. It was nice to catch up with Adelaide and Candace. They wanted to meet Rory, but they also insisted on holding the funeral at the library, so I had to turn them down. Adelaide has a daughter, too, Estelle. I wish Rory could meet her when she's a bit older...*

I lowered the journal, my eyes stinging. Who knew, maybe he'd have eventually introduced me to the library himself in defiance of the magical world's rules against bringing normals in, although when he'd done the same for his childhood friend, it'd backfired horribly. And Mum had died before she'd been given that chance...

A clattering noise sounded. I jerked upright, at first thinking Xavier was back, but the sound had come from somewhere among the shelves and not the door behind me.

I dropped the journal as I stood up, then I paced over to the nearest set of bookshelves. "Hello?"

No response came. It was possible I'd heard one of the books moving around or whispering, true, but it was too dark for me to see.

"What's up?" asked Xavier, making me jump. "Sorry, I shouldn't have startled you."

"Don't worry about it." I pressed a hand to my thumping heart. "I thought I saw something moving over here…"

"One of the books, do you think?" A soft thump sounded, and both of us spun in the direction of the door.

"Was that the door?" I strode back to where I'd left the journal and saw that the door to the fourth-floor corridor had closed, as if an unseen person had pulled it shut behind them.

Xavier glided past me and pulled the door open, peering upstairs. "Nobody's there."

"A draught?" I picked up the journal, which had flipped several pages forward. "I hope one of those biting books didn't get in there."

"Nah, we'd hear it climbing the stairs." He closed the door and then reached into his pocket, pulling out the bundle of keys I'd loaned him. "I tried all the keys, by the way, and none of them worked."

"Thanks anyway." I took the keys and sat down again. This time, I angled myself so that the door was within my sight instead of with my back to it. "They only work for family. Which probably includes Sylvester, but he's not willing to cooperate today."

"Can you convince Aunt Candace?" he suggested. "Not

that it would help matters if she got cursed twice over, but at least it wouldn't end in any new casualties."

Chills raced down my arms. "Not fond of that word."

"Sorry. Reaper. Force of habit."

"Yeah." I hitched on a smile. "This is one hell of a weird sleepover."

Despite my unease, part of me remained fascinated to know what was behind the doors. Strange, really. I wasn't a risk taker by nature, and I knew better than to toy with the library's unpredictable magic—yet with the door inches away, I couldn't help wondering if there was a way to safely to explore without getting cursed. Surely *looking* through the door wouldn't do any harm, right?

I rose to my feet again and faced the door. "Xavier, can you grab one of those lanterns?"

"Sure." He had to stand on tiptoe to reach the floating lantern, but he managed to pull it down. "You're not going in there?"

"No, but it'd be easier for us to see with more light." I pulled on the gloves I'd brought with me and then took the lantern from him. With my free hand, I pushed the door as widely open as it would go, holding up the lantern to peer upstairs.

Shadows shifted at the top. I inhaled sharply and leaned forward, but Xavier caught my arm. "Whoa, Rory."

I locked my feet to the spot, holding the lantern next to my face. "I thought I saw movement up there. Like... like someone's shadow."

Xavier glided through the door and climbed the stairs, the lantern's light illuminating his ascent. "Rory, there's nobody up here. Just a trick of the light."

Was it, though? Or is there something only I can see?

———

My dreams that night were full of endless corridors and shadowy, faceless figures disappearing out of sight. Over and over, I pushed open the door to the fourth-floor corridor and climbed the staircase. When I reached the top, I invariably saw an indistinct shadowy figure retreating around the corner, beckoning me to follow. When I rounded the corner, a door waited at the other end of the corridor, but the figure was gone.

That was usually when I woke up, but the last dream was different. This time, I reached out a hand, and the door flew open beneath my touch. Beyond was a room lined with bookshelves, and two figures sat in a pair of cosy armchairs in the centre.

My father and grandmother smiled at me. "Come in, Rory."

When I entered, the room changed, warping around me until it resembled the ballroom at Carlos Verdant's home. I reeled, surrounded by dancing vampires and human subjugates walking blank-faced among them, sweeping me along with the tide.

Trapped and desperate, I looked for a friendly face or a way out. My gaze snagged on someone familiar—*Dad*. He carried a tray of drinks, as blank-faced as the rest of the humans, and he didn't meet my eyes. I recoiled, and someone knocked into me. As I sidestepped, my gaze fell on the vampire leading the dance. An elderly woman with strong features.

Grandma.

I jerked awake to find myself in bed, the journal resting on my knees. "What the hell was that, subconscious?"

No response came—Xavier must have left at some point in the night, as he usually did—but with my dad's journal lying on top of me, it was no wonder he'd haunted my dreams. Him... and Grandma.

I gave myself a mental shake. I was fairly sure I'd know if either of them had become a vampire, and the dream was more likely to be some weird conjuration of my unconscious mind than a portent of doom. I'd spent half the night combing the journal's pages, both with Xavier's help and without, but all I'd found were some references to the library in general terms and nothing about the fourth floor.

Shaking off the dream, I got dressed and went downstairs. Nobody else was up yet, unusually, though Aunt Adelaide might have taken over from Estelle in guarding the fourth-floor-corridor door. I couldn't remember which time they'd agreed on.

"Partner." Jet fluttered over to me. "Your aunt still isn't interested in talking to me. She called me annoying!"

"She's not herself, Jet," I said absently. "We have to figure this one out today. Get the curse off her."

"What can I do, partner?"

Good question. I'd normally have a magic lesson in the morning, but since Aunt Candace was my teacher most of the time, that would have to be put on hold until we'd dealt with the curse. I could carry on working my way through the journal, but I'd pretty much resigned myself to finding nothing relating to the corridor.

As for Aunt Candace's notebook, I'd left it with Estelle. She'd had marginally more luck with deciphering our aunt's impenetrable handwriting than I had, though she had yet to look at the other notebooks in the research cave. Given the sheer volume of them, it would be a serious operation that would probably need several pairs of eyes. Unless we could get more clues from the woman herself.

"Is Estelle still up on the third floor?" I asked. "Or did she trade places with Aunt Adelaide?"

"I'll look, partner!" He zoomed off, his little feathery wings carrying him up to the balcony. I watched him, worry fluttering in my chest. I hoped Estelle had managed to stay awake throughout the night shift, preferably without any weird incidents like opening doors or strange noises. The rest of us would have heard if the manticore had escaped again, at least, but my experiences the previous night had left me decidedly on edge.

After a short pause, Jet came swooping downward and into the living room. "Cass is there, partner."

"Cass?" Had she and my aunt traded shifts? "Okay. I'll go up there. Can you watch and see if anyone comes downstairs?"

"Yes, partner!" He perched on the arm of the sofa while I left the living quarters and crossed the deserted lobby.

A booming voice came from behind the desk. "Where are you going?"

I tripped over my own feet and grabbed the desk to avoid face-planting. "Sylvester. You're back."

"Well observed." The owl stuck his head over the top of a bookcase. "And you're on your way upstairs for no good reason. Fancied a peek into the corridor, did you?"

"No, I…" I flushed. "I'm going to check on Cass. To see if anything happened last night while I was asleep."

"Really?" His head swivelled around in a manner that gave me vertigo. "Or is your curiosity getting the better of you?"

I debated mentioning the strange noises and mysteriously opening door, but he'd either make fun of me or dismiss me. Or fly off in a huff again at the reminder that he wasn't privy to the corridor's secrets. "I wanted to know why Cass is up there and not Aunt Adelaide."

"Your aunt has a library to run. Isn't that explanation enough?"

"I guess." Regardless, we really needed to make some decent progress today if we wanted to avoid the whole town finding out Aunt Candace had been cursed by one of our own corridors. "Did you find the book-wyrms?"

"Yes, and I ate them all." He closed his eyes. "And now, I plan to take a nap."

"Good for you." I heard movement from the living quarters as someone came downstairs. Leaving the owl, I met Aunt Adelaide in the living room.

"Hello, Rory," she said. "Did you sleep well?"

"Not really," I admitted. "Weird dreams. Oh—Sylvester's back. He seems to be in a less antagonistic mood today, but I didn't mention the corridor."

"Oh, good." She went into the kitchen and set about making breakfast. "I wonder if he'll volunteer to watch the door so the rest of us can have a break."

"I doubt it." I joined her, turning on the coffee maker. "Given how oversensitive he is that the corridor was hidden from him."

"True," she said. "It's a shame Xavier wasn't able to get any of those doors open."

"I know." I thought back to my dreams, and a shiver sprang to my arms. "I couldn't find anything in the journal, either, but I did hear… noises up there. And I kept thinking I saw someone moving around."

"Who?" she queried.

I shook my head. "I don't know, but the door kept opening by itself, without any explanation."

"It's a potently magical place, Rory," she said. "I'd be surprised if there *was* an explanation for anything that happens in there, except that my mother was more devious than I gave her credit for."

"Yeah." I paused, hearing more footsteps, and Aunt Candace entered the room.

"Hello there," she said cheerily. "Oh, you already made coffee. Marvelous."

"Uh-huh." I poured myself one and then did the same for my aunts. "Is Estelle asleep?"

"She is." Aunt Adelaide took a seat at the table. "She had a late night. So did I, for that matter."

"I slept wonderfully." Aunt Candace seized a slice of toast. "Despite the fascinating treasure trove of information upstairs."

"Good for you." Maybe it should have been an improvement, but it was like having an unpredictable stranger around, even if she was much cheerier than usual. As a result, I didn't feel comfortable bringing up the night's events again until we'd finished breakfast and she'd returned to her research cave.

"At least she has plenty to keep her occupied up there," Aunt Adelaide said. "It should stop her from getting into trouble while we figure out how to uncurse her."

"Any new ideas?" I asked.

"No." She yawned. "I was up half the night, looking up cases of curses that affected people after the caster's death, and it's almost always because the curse was placed upon an object. Most were resolved by destroying the object in question."

"Then how would we go about undoing this one?" I asked. "I mean, we don't actually want to destroy the corridor, if it's even possible."

"No, and even if it was, the corridor itself might not be the source," she said. "The curse might be on a single object in there that your aunt touched."

"I don't know that there was anything for her to touch except for the doors," I replied. "Or those mirrors, maybe. I could ask Xavier..."

"No," she said. "We can't afford for any more of us to end up cursed, Rory, and there's no telling what the limits are.

For all we know, simply removing the object from the corridor will trigger another reaction."

"Oh." My shoulders slumped. "I hoped one of us would come up with an idea if we slept on it. I know Estelle was reading Aunt Candace's notebook, but she didn't unearth anything in there."

"No, and I actually went into my sister's research cave last night while she was sleeping," said Aunt Adelaide. "I checked the notebooks that she regularly uses, but there weren't any references to the corridor. Not one."

"Weird." Had she made the notes on her computer or in another notebook that she'd left elsewhere? Or had Lisa Grubbins swiped more than one notebook? "Maybe they're on her computer."

"If so, we won't find them," she said. "My sister has trouble remembering her passwords on a good day."

"Ah." I grimaced. "Well, there's always the chance that Lisa Grubbins is the one who found the corridor instead."

"No, she can't possibly know," she said. "I looked *her* up, and she's been away from town the past decade. She only moved back when she got engaged."

"I figured from the state of their house," I replied, "but I don't trust her. Either of them."

"No." She walked out of the kitchen. "I'll see if Sylvester is willing to look around up on the third floor to see if we missed anything. I can trust you to watch the desk in the meantime, can't I, Rory?"

"Of course." I headed for the front desk, racking my mind for more ideas. Opening the library as usual seemed risky, but since we didn't know how long it would take to resolve the curse, it was the best way forward. *I hope.*

As I settled behind the desk, someone knocked on the door. Loudly.

Tensing, I waited for an instant, and another loud knock

prompted me to hurry to the front door. On the other side, I found none other than Jamie, the rat-faced wizard, standing in the entryway.

My heart gave a lurch at the sight of him. "Erm. Can I help you?"

His eyes roved around the library with marked contempt. "My fiancée is missing."

9

*L*isa Grubbins is missing?

My mouth parted. "What do you mean?"

"I thought you knew what words mean, being a librarian." He sneered. "She's *missing*. And it's because you did something to her."

"I didn't do anything," I said. "I haven't seen her either. You're the first person who's come into the library today."

His hand clenched. "You're a liar. You and your cousin did something to her yesterday."

"I really didn't." I backed up a few steps until my feet hit the front of the desk, and then, to my relief, Aunt Adelaide came back into view.

"Is there a problem?" she asked.

"Aunt Adelaide," I said. "Ah—I think something happened to Lisa. He said she's missing, but she definitely didn't come here, did she?"

"Of course she didn't." She stepped forward, facing Jamie. "Missing? When did this happen?"

"In the middle of the night," he growled. "She disappeared. Sneaked out without telling me a thing."

"Is that... I mean, has she ever done that before?" I regretted the question instantly when he clenched his fist again.

"No, it certainly isn't normal," he snarled. "She isn't at work. She isn't anywhere. I want you to give her back."

"She isn't here," said Aunt Adelaide. "The library is fitted with alarms that alert us whenever anyone tries to get in, and we have security watching the place overnight."

By "security," she meant Sylvester, who wouldn't have let anyone into the library even as a joke. Not that we could count on the owl jumping to our defence given his current erratic mood.

"Then tell me what you did to her," Jamie went on. "I know something was funny here yesterday. Lisa herself told me there was a curse."

My heart jumped. *How did she know?* She hadn't seen Aunt Candace when she'd fallen under the spell, had she? Unless she *had* still been upstairs at the time, and she'd taken advantage of our aunt's confusion to swipe her notebook from under her nose. For all I knew, that was exactly how she'd obtained it.

"Wherever Lisa is, the library had nothing to do with it," Aunt Adelaide said firmly. "I'm sure she'll have a reasonable explanation."

"A likely story." He pointed his wand at both of us. "Lisa told me all about your family's lies. You're notorious for them. That's why I'm prepared. Want to tell me the truth, or should I loosen your tongues in my own way?"

Before anyone could move an inch, Sylvester came swooping down and landed on the front desk. "And who might you be?"

Jamie jumped, nearly dropping his wand. "You... you're talking."

"This one isn't very bright, is he?" Sylvester remarked.

The wizard flushed a furious red. "Now your animals are insulting me?"

Oh boy. If he attacked Sylvester… well, as entertaining as it might be to see the owl chase him off or trap him in the Forbidden Room, that wouldn't help the situation in the slightest.

"Sylvester is our security," said Aunt Adelaide. "He would have seen if your fiancée came near the library and alerted us at once."

"Has a fiancée, does he?" said the owl. "Well, there's no accounting for taste."

I groaned inwardly as Jamie's face turned to more of a mauve colour. "I won't stand for this!"

"Sylvester," I said out of the corner of my mouth. "His fiancée is missing, and he seems to think we were involved."

I figured Sylvester had already heard the rest, but antagonising the wizard wouldn't end favourably for the library when he was already going around spreading rumours about curses. Even if those rumours were true.

"I want you to give me back my future wife!" Jamie shouted, spittle flying from his mouth. "I know you were involved."

The owl studied him with disdain. "Lost her, did you? That was careless of you."

"*Sylvester.*"

Jamie raised his wand again, and the owl spread his wings threateningly.

An instant later, there came a deafening roar from upstairs. The wizard jumped violently, lifting his head to see where the noise had come from.

Not to be outdone, Sylvester beat his wings, sending a gust of wind towards the wizard. "Get out."

Panic spread over Jamie's face, and with one final look of fury at all of us, he ran out of the library. The door slammed shut behind him, and upstairs, the manticore gave another roar.

"Not again." I ran for the stairs up to the balcony and began to climb, barely stopping to breathe until I reached the third floor.

I skidded to a halt in front of the door to the Magical Creatures Division, which Cass was in the process of closing on the manticore. "You're welcome."

"Wait, you let it out on purpose this time?" I blinked. "Did you hear everything?"

"No, but I saw that guy pick a fight with Sylvester."

"He's Lisa Grubbins's fiancé," I said. "She went missing last night."

"Am I supposed to care?"

"Cass, Lisa was up here with Aunt Candace." I gestured at the hammock where she'd been sitting. "She also stole her notebook and then tried to curse Estelle and me when we took it back."

"Did she get herself cursed by the corridor too?" She paced back to the door she'd been watching, which was a vibrant green colour today. "Serves her right."

"I don't know that she's cursed." After last night's dreams, I was doubly wary of the closed door, but Cass's unflappable demeanour suggested it hadn't played any tricks on her so far. The door didn't look half as ominous in the full daylight as it had last night either. "She must have seen Aunt Candace yesterday, though, when she stole the notebook."

"Are you sure *she* didn't curse her, not the corridor?"

"You think Lisa's the one who cursed Aunt Candace?" I frowned, not having thought of that possibility. "If she did, it doesn't explain why she's gone missing."

"Guilty conscience?" she suggested.

"I don't think so, somehow." From what I'd seen of both her *and* Jamie, they were lacking in scruples to say the least. "There's a good chance the corridor is involved, and we haven't done ourselves any favours by fighting with her future husband."

"Does that surprise you?" she said. "Estelle didn't mention seeing anyone come into the library last night, and I didn't see anyone either. That guy needs to get a life."

"At least we can agree on that."

I went downstairs again, thinking hard. If the corridor had cursed Lisa after all, it surely wasn't the same as the curse on Aunt Candace given the time delay. If she'd been into the corridor herself and touched anything, it was entirely possible that she'd picked up a different curse altogether, but there was no way to prove it when Lisa and Jamie themselves certainly wouldn't admit to anything. All we could do was wait and see if she showed up at the library.

Aunt Adelaide agreed. When the library opened for the day, we both remained at the front desk, taking it in turns to help patrons find the books they needed. From the ground floor, nothing seemed to be amiss, though I remained on tenterhooks all morning, expecting Jamie to show up again.

Instead, an unpleasant surprise arrived midmorning in the form of Edwin and his two troll bodyguards. The elf who ran the town's police force walked into the lobby, wearing the long-suffering expression he reserved for dealing with Aunt Candace.

"I've had a report of a missing person in connection with your library," he said.

Aunt Adelaide grimaced. "Yes, Jamie came here to claim that his fiancée went missing last night. She didn't come into the library, but we're keeping an eye out for her."

"He also claims she got cursed here." His eyes narrowed. "I'm hearing all kinds of rumours about people being banned from the third floor."

"We found the missing door to the fourth-floor corridor yesterday," said Aunt Adelaide. "And a book-wyrm infestation, which is why we initially closed off access to the third floor."

"A *missing* corridor?"

"Yes, until my sister found it," she said. "Unfortunately, the corridor had some kind of defensive mechanism that caused her to lose her memories, as you may have heard from Mr Bennet."

"The curse-breaker?" he asked. "I realise your family has lapses in judgement sometimes, but if members of the public are going missing, I'm going to need you to be honest with me."

"Lisa didn't go missing here," I said quickly. "She *was* here yesterday when the door was discovered, but only Aunt Candace ended up cursed, and that's because she went through the door herself. I don't know if Lisa did the same."

"Did she now?" Edwin said. "Have you informed the public of this?"

"We've closed the third floor until we can determine what happened yesterday," said Aunt Adelaide, "but as of yet, there's no proof the corridor is a danger to anyone. We've had a member of our family watching it carefully ever since it was discovered yesterday."

"By your sister—who ended up cursed." His mouth twisted in a scowl. "This puts your family in a difficult position, as you ought to know."

"Lisa Grubbins stole Aunt Candace's notebook while she was incapacitated," I told him. "She and Aunt Candace were rivals at school, though my aunt currently has no memory of any of that. Only Lisa does."

"They have a history, do they?"

"She and Candace had a dispute a long time ago," Aunt Adelaide said. "I sent Rory and Estelle to ask her a few questions to find out if she witnessed anything up on the third floor. They found that Lisa had stolen my sister's notebook, and they retrieved it."

"Neither of us cursed her," I added. "She and Jamie tried to curse *us* when we took the notebook back. He also came here and threatened the library. That's why we kicked him out."

"I see," he said. "I do hope you haven't omitted any details. This man is threatening legal action, and he seems to have a valid case."

"If Lisa did go into the corridor yesterday, it's possible she was cursed in a similar way to my sister," said Aunt Adelaide. "However, we haven't seen any sign of her today, and we will not accept any threats against the library or our family."

Edwin sighed. "You go out of your way to make my life difficult, don't you?"

"Not on purpose," I protested. "I really don't know where Lisa is, but there are only so many places someone can go missing in a town this small, right?"

"Yes, there are," he said. "I sincerely hope you're being honest with me. I'll resume the search elsewhere."

As he and the trolls left the library, I turned to my aunt. "We've got to figure this one out. Cass put forward the possibility that Lisa is the one who cursed Aunt Candace, not the corridor."

"Did she?" She frowned. "That's one theory, but it doesn't explain why Lisa is missing."

"No." It didn't, and neither did any other theory I could think of. "I don't know why she stole Aunt Candace's notebook in the first place, except out of pettiness, but this Jamie seems to be pushing the curse theory hard. Maybe he does know more than he let on."

"Does Estelle still have the notebook?" she asked.

"I can check, but she's probably asleep," I said. "I thought she didn't find anything in there."

"Yes, but—well…" She paused for an instant. "It's *possible* that my sister put a defensive spell on the notebook that retaliates against anyone who tries to steal it."

"She didn't, did she?" It did sound just like my aunt, unfortunately. "Wait—*I* touched the notebook when I seized it back. So did Estelle. That ought to mean it's okay, right?"

"Yes, that's true." She rubbed her eyes, looking tired. "We don't need any more bad publicity, and I'm wary of any possible angle Jamie can use against us. Can you go and ask Estelle for the notebook?"

"Sure." I headed for the corridor to the living quarters and then climbed the staircase to the corridor where our rooms were located. Then I walked past my own room, reached her door, and knocked.

After a short pause, Estelle answered, bleary-eyed and yawning. "Hey, Rory. Sorry… I was so tired I passed out as soon as I got back to my room."

"At least you have your memories."

She ran the back of her hand over her eyes. "Yes. Why wouldn't I?"

"Your mother wanted to know if you still have Aunt Candace's notebook."

She blinked. "I left it on the third floor for Cass."

"Did you?" I hadn't seen it when I'd been upstairs, but I hadn't known to pay attention. "We have a bit of a crisis on our hands. Lisa is missing, and her future husband came to threaten the library."

"He didn't, did he?" Her eyes widened; she was now wide awake. "Does he think we were involved?"

"Pretty much," I said. "I don't know if she's cursed, like Aunt Candace, but the time delay made your mum wonder if Aunt Candace's notebook had a defensive spell on it. I figured it would have affected both of us if it did, but I wanted to check."

"Oh." Her brow furrowed. "I don't think so. I feel fine. Just tired."

"Same," I said. "I think we're all a little paranoid, but Cass suggested that Lisa is the one who cursed Aunt Candace, not the corridor. Not that there's any way to confirm one way or another as long as she's missing."

"We have good reason to be paranoid," she said. "If the corridor is cursing people who aren't even in the library... unless Aunt Candace sneaked out in the middle of the night and cursed her."

"You know, if she wasn't under a curse herself, I might suspect her of doing exactly that." I shook my head. "But she doesn't even remember who Lisa is."

"How is she today?"

"Aunt Candace? Same as yesterday," I replied. "She's in her research cave. Your mum went in there last night and checked the notebooks that Aunt Candace regularly uses, but she didn't find anything on the corridor. So unless she made notes digitally..."

"Yeah... *that's* weird," Estelle said. "I can get the notebook from upstairs and carry on scouring for clues. I'm not going to get any more sleep while my head is spinning like this."

"I know the feeling." I backed down the corridor to the stairs and then climbed to the topmost floor.

When I knocked on the door to Aunt Candace's research cave, she came to the door with another vague smile. "Hello, Rory."

My mind went blank. "Erm... I just wondered what you were doing."

"Oh, I was reading these articles." She gestured to the shelves behind her. "There's a wealth of fascinating material in here, and an awful lot of it is related to mysterious deaths and other incidents. It's as if the person who set up this place personally knew me."

Hmm. The curse hadn't changed that part of her basic personality, evidently, but I didn't believe someone with this level of wide-eyed innocence would have cursed Lisa. "Aunt Candace, did you see Lisa Grubbins yesterday?"

"Who?"

"Lisa." *Nope, she still doesn't remember.* "She was on the third floor when you were, erm, cursed. Anyway, she's gone missing."

"Missing?" Her eyes gleamed. "Ooh, a mystery. Do you want my help to solve it?"

"Sure, why not." It'd give her something to do if nothing else. "Can you note down everything you remember from the third floor yesterday?"

She deflated. "I told you, I don't remember. I wish I did, but I don't have anything else to say."

My gaze fell on her laptop, which lay on a chair in the corner. "Can I borrow your laptop?"

"This is mine?" she asked. "I assumed it was someone else's."

"No, it's yours… but none of us knows what the password is." I figured the detail hadn't slipped by her memory spell. "You might have written it down somewhere. If you find any scraps of paper while you're researching, can you let me know?"

"Of course." Her vague smile returned, and I walked out of the room as she vanished behind the shelves, humming to herself.

Downstairs, I returned to Aunt Adelaide at the front desk.

"Estelle gave the notebook to Cass," I told her. "Also, Aunt

Candace can't recall any more details from yesterday. Or her computer password, either, presumably."

"As I expected," Aunt Adelaide said. "I suppose we can ask the curse-breaker to have a look at her notebook to be on the safe side, but it's unlikely for it to have cursed Lisa and not you or Estelle."

"Yeah, Aunt Candace wouldn't make an exception for family," I said. "I don't think she'll be able to help us find Lisa either."

At that moment, the front door flew open, and Lisa Grubbins herself walked into the library. She looked completely different than the day before, dressed in jeans and a bright shirt that looked as if she'd pulled them out of the wardrobe of someone twenty years younger than her. She also looked like she'd slept on the floor, which she probably had if she'd run out of her house in the middle of the night.

Aunt Adelaide recovered from her shock before I did. "Can I help you?"

"This the library?" She scanned the lower floor with a mixture of disdain and incredulity. "It's bigger than I remember."

"You were here yesterday," I said. "Erm—do you remember who you are?"

"Do I remember what?" She eyed me. "You're one of Candace's siblings, are you? Did she tell you to make fun of me?"

"You know Candace?" Aunt Adelaide asked.

"Yes, we went to the same school," she said. "You must be her mother."

Huh? "No, she… wait. How old are you?"

She lifted her chin. "Eighteen, of course. Old enough to be here by myself. I want a book."

"You want… a book?" Had her memories somehow been catapulted several decades into the past? "Which book?"

I couldn't figure out what to do other than to play along, but if her future husband showed up again, the odds were high that Lisa would have forgotten his existence altogether. *This is not going to end well.*

10

Lisa made for the Reading Corner with a surprising lack of argument. She might not have been a fan of Aunt Candace, but she didn't seem quite as disagreeable as she had in her previous incarnation. Not that that would save us from the wrath of her future husband when he inevitably found out she was here.

Estelle came into the lobby and did a double take when she saw Lisa's retreating back. "She showed up?"

"She lost her memory," I told her in an undertone. "If the corridor was responsible, it didn't take as many memories as it did with Aunt Candace."

"It took enough," said Aunt Adelaide. "She seems to think she's a university student, which means she most likely won't recognise her fiancé if he comes back."

"Yeah… that's a problem." How were we supposed to undo the curse in the time it took for Jamie to realise where she was? "If we go by the assumption that the corridor cursed her like with Aunt Candace, that's got to be where the answers are."

"Precisely," said Aunt Adelaide. "My mother's security

measures are responsible for this, and I would wager they're designed to prevent anyone telling tales about what's behind that door."

"But—that shifter, Walter," said Estelle. "*He* went into the corridor as well."

"We'll have to check on him later," said Aunt Adelaide. "Xavier and Laney are immune, though. Don't look so worried, Rory."

"I know, but they told *me* what they saw in there," I said. "Laney even drew a map."

"That's true," Estelle said anxiously. "We all know exactly what Xavier saw. Laney too. Is it just physical touch that triggers the curse, do you think?"

"Might be if Lisa went in there too," I said. "Pity we can't rely on her to remember doing it—or Aunt Candace either."

"Walter might remember," Estelle suggested. "Not that he had much to say yesterday."

"He's our last remaining lead who might have his memories of the events," said Aunt Adelaide. "I'd say one of us ought to talk to him."

"I guess," said Estelle. "I'll see if I can find his phone number or address, but I *hope* he isn't cursed as well."

As she backed away to make the call, I tensed when the front door opened, but it was only Xavier.

"Rory." His gaze searched me, concerned. "What's this about someone threatening you?"

Oh, right. I'd sent him a message earlier, explaining what was going on. "Lisa's future husband blamed us for her going missing, but now she's shown up at the library without any memories of the last twenty or so years. She thinks she's a university student."

"Seriously?"

"Yep," I said. "Needless to say, we aren't Jamie's favourite people. Sylvester already had to chase him out of the library."

His expression shadowed. "He shouldn't be allowed to threaten you."

"We *did* get his future wife cursed." I watched as Estelle walked back into view, frowning at her phone. "Any luck with Walter?"

"He's not answering the phone," she said. "And he didn't turn up at work either. I did find his address, though. He lives in an apartment near the university campus."

"Who?" asked Xavier.

"Walter," I replied. "The shifter you rescued from the fourth floor. We were wondering if he got cursed too."

"Should we go and check up on him?" Xavier asked. "I don't mind going with you for moral support if Lisa's fiancé is out there."

"Yeah… it's only a matter of time before he comes back." I turned to Aunt Adelaide. "Is that okay?"

"Of course." She nodded to Estelle. "We'll watch things here. Make sure that Jamie doesn't start causing trouble. If you see Edwin, can you let him know Lisa is here?"

"Good idea." I got the shifter's address from Estelle, and then Xavier and I left the library.

Mercifully, Jamie was nowhere to be seen and neither were Edwin or his troll guards. It was possible that the former was at the police station, pestering the latter, but we had to find Walter the shifter before we dealt with anything else.

As we crossed the square, I told Xavier the rest of the recent developments, including our lack of luck with finding clues about Aunt Candace's knowledge of the corridor prior to her being cursed.

"Weird," he said. "Might she have made notes elsewhere?"

"Aunt Adelaide checked the obvious places," I said. "And she doesn't remember her laptop passwords. Of course, there's always the possibility that Lisa stole more than one notebook, but short of breaking and entering while Jamie isn't around…"

"Tricky," he said. "That Jamie strikes me as just as much of a troublemaker. Maybe they're both involved."

"It'd save us a lot of hassle if he lost his memories too." Not that he'd been near the corridor, and I intended to keep it that way. "I wish I knew how the curse even worked. Some curses have an inbuilt delay, but Aunt Candace was affected right away. It makes no sense for Lisa not to be."

"That's the curse-breaker's area, right?" He turned up the high street, and we followed the quickest route to the university campus. "Curses are unpredictable at the best of times, and when you add the library's magic on top of that, it's no wonder even he struggled to find answers."

"Tell me about it." I heaved a sigh. "Even Sylvester couldn't figure it out. Though he did send Jamie packing."

"That ought to keep him from coming back."

"Not if he finds out Lisa's in there." I checked the address I'd inputted into my phone and turned onto the right street. "Besides, it won't endear us to the police if we sent an owl to chase them both off."

We reached the apartment block in which Walter lived, and I rang the buzzer for the right flat. Nobody answered, and after a few moments, I tried again, with the same result.

"Which floor?" Xavier peered at the row of windows in front and then startled. "Whoa. There's a werewolf in there."

I followed his gaze. Through a gap in the curtains of one of the ground-floor flats, a large wolf lay curled up on the floor.

"That's the same guy… right?" It wasn't the full moon, and shifters didn't randomly turn into their animal forms in their own homes, according to my admittedly limited experience. "I wonder if anyone else has seen him since he came to the library."

"I'll check." Xavier vanished into the shadows, and the front door to the building opened a moment later. Really, it was a good job Reapers were bound by a code of conduct, because they'd have made expert burglars. He'd bypassed the security doors in a heartbeat, opening them from the inside to let me in.

"I don't know about this," I whispered. "I don't want to break into that guy's apartment."

"We don't have to," he said. "I thought we could question his neighbours, and you're less likely to frighten people than I am."

I forced a laugh. "I guess. I'm no detective, though… and Edwin's not going to be pleased with us if he finds out."

With the chance that Jamie was at the police station, we couldn't risk going there for help. Besides, there might be nothing wrong after all, and Walter might like turning into a werewolf in his free time. And be an unreliable employee. Who knew?

With the distinct feeling that I was crossing a line, I helped Xavier find the door that corresponded to the window through which we'd seen the wolf from outside. When I knocked on the door, nobody answered, as I'd expected.

"Let's try this one." Xavier moved to the apartment next door and rapped on the wooden surface.

A young woman wearing a tiger onesie answered the door. "Can I help you?"

I hastily moved to Xavier's side in case she recognised him as the Reaper and freaked out. "Sorry to disturb you, but I wondered if you've seen your neighbour recently. Walter."

"Not since yesterday," she said. "Why?"

"He never showed up at work," I said. "He isn't answering his phone either. And we saw through the window… well, he's in the form of a wolf."

She blinked. "I don't know him that well, but he doesn't normally shift into wolf form unless it's the full moon."

Unless he panicked. Like at the library. "You don't mind if we check up on him, do you?"

"Me?" she asked. "No. Like I said, I don't know him. I've heard of shifters getting stuck in animal form, though. He might appreciate the help."

"Yeah, that's what I figured," I said. "Thanks anyway."

I waited for her to withdraw into her flat before I returned to Walter's door and knocked for a third time.

"From the window, he looked like he was asleep," Xavier commented. "I can try to get his attention…"

An audible growl came from the other side of the door, and I jumped. "I think we already did."

The door rattled in its frame. *Uh-oh.*

Xavier grabbed my arm. "We should go."

"Agreed." I turned away as the growling became a full-blown roar. "Someone didn't like being woken up from his nap."

The door crashed open behind us, and the werewolf came charging out into the corridor. As I ran, I reached for my wand and pointed it wildly over my shoulder, casting the first spell that came to mind—a lullaby charm.

The werewolf stopped mid-charge and slumped to the floor, landing inches from my heels. Thanking the hours I'd spent practising for the next time I had to outrun a vampire, I caught my breath, while several of the other flats' inhabitants goggled at us from their doorways.

"Sorry," I gasped out. "He's—I don't know what's wrong with him, but I think he might be trapped in animal form."

Someone was already on their phone, calling the police or possibly an ambulance. Either way, we wouldn't help matters by sticking around.

As we left the building, Xavier swore under his breath. "I'm sorry, Rory. I didn't expect him to react like that."

"If he got cursed into animal form, he's bound to be a little jumpy," I commented. "What I'd like to know is if it's the same curse that hit Aunt Candace and Lisa. All three were affected differently."

"Were they?" He took my hand as we walked, heading for the high street. "Two of them lost their memories, and for all we know, Walter did too."

"If he lost his memories, it's no wonder he panicked when we showed up at his flat."

Not that there was any way to communicate with a shifter in their animal form. Not for a human, anyway. But something didn't add up. Lisa and Aunt Candace had both lost their memories, true, but they'd been affected in such drastically different ways that it was hard to see it as the result of the same curse.

"A shifter can question him, can't they?" Xavier said. "Maybe we should contact the head of the werewolf pack."

"Definitely not," I said firmly. "There are enough rumours circulating already without us showing up at the chief's house."

"Rumours from Lisa and her fiancé, right?" asked Xavier. "She lost her memories… but only the recent ones?"

"The last twenty-something years," I replied. "While Aunt Candace seems to have lost all sense of herself altogether. My Aunt Adelaide's theory is that it's a security spell that's intended to stop anyone talking about what's in the corridor…"

"That's got to be it," Xavier said. "Your Aunt Candace was researching the fourth floor for years, but that Lisa only took a recent interest. That's why your aunt lost more memories than Lisa did."

"It's not supposed to be possible for a curse to be that

specific." I thought back to the movement I'd seen last night, the strange noises, and the way the door seemed to open and close of its own accord. As if someone was leaving. "Unless… unless someone from the corridor is casting different curses on everyone who trespasses in there."

"Who?" His brow crinkled. "If someone was in there, I'd have seen them."

"I know." We reached the library's doorstep. "I don't know what to think. I hope someone can get some sense out of Walter."

"I'll keep an eye out and let you know," he said. "Please be careful. If that Jamie shows up again, tell me, okay?"

"Will do."

I went back into the library to find Estelle and Aunt Adelaide and told them of Walter's unfortunate state.

"How can the curse have trapped him in the form of an animal?" asked Estelle. "That sounds like more of a shifter-specific curse. Unless it was the shock."

"He was fine when he left the library, wasn't he?" I asked. "I don't know how specific curses can get, but it's already had different effects on both Aunt Candace and Lisa too. Where is she now?"

"Still in the Reading Corner," Estelle replied. "I should check up on her, but I forgot to. I did go upstairs, but Cass can't find Aunt Candace's notebook either."

"It's missing again?" I frowned. "Lisa didn't take it?"

"Can't be," she said. "Nobody can get to the third floor, including her. Besides, it's been missing since before she got here."

"Where is Walter now?" Aunt Adelaide asked.

"Lying unconscious in the corridor of his apartment building," I said. "He tried to chase off Xavier and me, and I used a lullaby charm to keep him from trampling us. I expect

Edwin will give me grief over that. At least one person was calling the authorities when we left."

Aunt Adelaide's gaze clouded. "One of us should go there to wait for the police in case there's anything we can do to help."

"Xavier's there," I explained. "But we didn't go to the police ourselves in case that Jamie was hanging around the station, waiting for news on his fiancée. That's why I don't think we should leave the library either."

"He'll have to try harder than that to intimidate me." Aunt Adelaide straightened her shoulders. "You can watch Lisa while I'm gone, can't you?"

"Of course," Estelle said. "We'll make sure she stays out of trouble."

As my aunt left the library, I heard a commotion from the Reading Corner. "Famous last words."

Bracing myself, I hurried through the stacks. In the studying area near the Reading Corner, Lisa stood on a desk, holding up what appeared to be a long dress to display to everyone in the vicinity.

"This dress is equipped with a spell that will remove all wrinkles for the rest of your life," she told a group of students at a nearby table. "It's the genuine deal."

"Doesn't look like it to me," said one of the students. "It clearly hasn't worked on you."

"Well, it can't make you any less ugly, can it?" she retaliated.

"Oh boy," I muttered. "Was this what she was like as a student too?"

"Selling dodgy spells to her fellow students sounds exactly like her," Estelle agreed. "Ah—excuse me? Lisa?"

She scowled at us over the top of the dress. "What?"

"You can't sell to the public inside the library," Estelle told her. "It's against the rules."

"Says who?"

"Us," said Estelle. "You can stay in here, but no more pitching your products to the students."

Lisa flushed in anger when several students snickered at her, and she hopped off the table. "I'm never coming here again."

To the visible relief of everyone around her, she marched out of the Reading Corner. My heart dropped when she approached the front door. *What if Jamie is outside?*

"Wait a moment." I hastened to catch up to her. "Where are you going?"

"Back to campus. Where else?"

Uh-oh. If she went to the university, thinking she still lived there, there was a good chance she'd end up trying to break into someone else's accommodation. I gave an alarmed glance at Estelle, who said, "Wait, you don't have to leave."

"Don't I?" She glared at us. "Candace put you up to this, didn't she? I bet she's hiding in here, laughing at me."

"Why do you dislike my aunt so much?" I asked, out of any other ideas as to how to prevent her from running off. "What did she do?"

Aunt Candace wasn't a published author yet in Lisa's mind, which meant Lisa had yet to receive the dubious honour of being killed off in a book.

"What did she do?" she echoed. "What *didn't* she do? She was always using me as a guinea pig for her ridiculous spells. She made my hair fall out once."

Oh boy. That sounded like Aunt Candace. She didn't need to be writing books to make trouble.

"We don't know about any spells," said Estelle, "but I can go and get her if you want to talk to her."

"Don't you even think about telling tales to her." Lisa reached up her sleeve and pulled out her wand. "Your whole family is trouble. And your library too."

Estelle raised her hands placatingly. "We can talk. There's no need for anyone to lose their temper."

As Lisa lifted her wand, I reached for my own. For the second time that day, I cast a swift lullaby charm. Lisa slumped on the floor, her wand slipping from her hand.

"That's better." Estelle picked up Lisa's wand. "She was a nasty piece of work even as a student."

"It doesn't sound like Aunt Candace was much better." I lowered my wand. "What are we supposed to do with her now?"

"Take her home?" she suggested. "I think it's the only place she might stay out of trouble."

"Assuming Jamie isn't there." If he was, we'd only land ourselves in deeper trouble. "No—we'll have to call Edwin and explain. She was technically breaking the law by trying to curse us and selling spelled clothing, even if she didn't know what she was doing. He might want to talk to her himself."

"He won't get much sense out of her, I bet." She reached for her phone then hesitated. "He might still be with Walter. We need the curse-breaker, ideally, but I don't know that there's anything more he can do for—"

As luck would have it, the library door opened, and Jamie himself walked in, stopping short at the sight of his future wife lying unconscious on the floor. "What the hell is this?"

"We found Lisa," I explained. "She came into the library and thought she was a student. We had to—"

"What did you do to her?" His eyes bulged out of his face. "You drugged her!"

"It was a lullaby charm," I said quickly. "She was about to curse both of us, but we didn't hurt her. She'll wake up soon."

"A likely story." He jumped when a violent hooting noise came from upstairs—Sylvester's reminder that we weren't without our own defences. "You and your library will pay for this."

He lifted Lisa in his arms and carried her out of the library, the door swinging shut behind him.

"We should report him to Edwin," said Estelle after a tense pause. "In case he does come back."

"And tell him we knocked out his fiancée?"

She winced. "Good point, but what else was there to do? She wasn't going to calm down willingly."

"I know." Guilt twinged in my chest all the same. Considering we were responsible for getting her cursed to begin with, Jamie's anger at the library was entirely justified, and Edwin would probably agree.

I tensed when the door opened again, but it was just Aunt Adelaide. "Was that Jamie? He was carrying Lisa…"

"She was harassing the students by trying to sell them dodgy spelled clothing," I explained. "I had to use a lullaby spell to stop her from cursing us, and her future husband didn't take it well."

She swore under her breath. "Edwin isn't pleased with Walter's condition either. He brought in a couple of shifters to question him in werewolf form, but Walter's only replying in barks."

"What—he thinks he's an actual wolf?" Estelle blinked at her mother. "Seriously?"

"The consensus is that he's forgotten he's human at all," she said. "He's currently under supervision until the cursebreaker pays a visit, but I don't know that he'll be able to do anything without bringing him back to the library."

"But—we haven't found anything here either," I said. "Not even what's in that corridor."

Estelle pointed towards the living quarters. "We could always ask her."

I swivelled that way and saw Aunt Candace hovering in

the doorway. Her flowery dress made her almost look like her old self if not for the vague expression on her face. "Ask me what?"

"About the fourth-floor corridor," I said. "The place you ended up cursed."

"Cursed?" she echoed. "I told you, I don't remember any of that."

"Never mind," I said. "Aunt Adelaide, did she ever mention using Lisa as her target for experimental spells that made her hair fall out?"

My aunt groaned. "Yes, she did. Is that what set Lisa off?"

"Are you whispering about me behind my back again?" Aunt Candace looked peeved. "I don't appreciate it."

We were wasting our time trying to get answers from her, I knew, but I still had to wonder how close Lisa had got to the corridor. She might not have been hit as badly as Aunt Candace and Walter had, but she must have been close enough that the security spell had reacted against her.

Yet everything we'd seen suggested that she'd left the library not long after Aunt Candace had been cursed, and she'd seemed normal enough when Estelle and I had visited yesterday. How, then, had she ended up cursed?

The shadowy figure I'd seen entered my mind's eye. If there *was* someone inside the corridor, human or otherwise, who could leave if they wanted, it wouldn't be impossible for them to have tracked down both Walter and Lisa after they'd already left the library. Was the security on the corridor not a curse but a person, capable of adapting the curses they cast on trespassers depending on how much their target had seen? If so, how could we track them down?

11

Leaving Aunt Adelaide to talk to her sister, I beckoned Estelle aside. "I have a theory about the curse."

"What theory?"

"I think the curse is moving around." I struggled to put my half-formed ideas into words, but to find more certainty, I needed someone else's input. "It hit both Walter and Lisa when they weren't in the library. Unless they each picked up a different curse with a similar delayed effect, either there's a person in there acting as security, or the curse itself is sentient and has a physical form of some kind."

"What?" she said. "No, that's impossible. Curses aren't sentient."

"I know," I said, "but Lisa and Walter were both cursed *after* being in the library, and the effects are way too different to be the same curse."

"I don't know about that," she said. "Don't get me wrong; I want to know what cursed them too, but I'd be surprised if Edwin isn't on his way here soon to question us. That's what we should be focused on."

"We need to pin down the curse's location to undo it, don't we?" Worry twisted in my chest at the mention of Edwin and the reminder that Jamie was out there too. "If it has more than one location or if it's moving around, that's going to be doubly difficult."

"I thought the corridor itself was the source." Her forehead scrunched up. "Which is problem enough when we can't go in there ourselves, of course."

"One of us can." I indicated the living room, where Aunt Candace sat. "She's already cursed, and she's family, so she'll be able to use the keys. I don't know how else we can find out what's in there."

"That strikes me as a risky idea." She eyed her mother and aunt. "Though being inside the corridor again might trigger her memories too. I wonder…"

"What is it?" Aunt Adelaide crossed the lobby from the living quarters, where she'd left Aunt Candace in an armchair with a book. "Did you have an idea?"

"Not a very good one," I admitted. "I thought Aunt Candace could have a look around the corridor again. Since she's already cursed, she might not trip the alarm this time, and she might be able to find out what cursed Lisa and Walter."

Aunt Adelaide sucked in a breath. "That's true, but it's risky, given my sister's vulnerable state."

"I know," I said, "but what better way to jog her memory than to take her back to the source?"

Let's face it—staying away from the corridor altogether wasn't doing any of us any favours. To find the truth, one of us would have to offer ourselves as bait and go inside, and unfortunately for Aunt Candace, she was the one least likely to be further affected by the corridor.

"I'll ask her." Aunt Adelaide walked over to her sister, and I followed her across the lobby. "Candace, Rory wondered if you'd like to go back to look around the fourth-floor corridor."

Aunt Candace looked up from her book—one of her own romance titles, in fact—and frowned. "Didn't you just say the fourth floor was dangerous?"

"It's where you got cursed," I said, "but we think the solution might be up there too. Would you like to go and help us look around?"

"Well, all right." She bounded to her feet. "Shall we be off?"

I hadn't expected her to agree so readily, though she'd been excited at the prospect of exploring the rest of the library. At least one person was being cooperative, though I began to have doubts as soon as Aunt Candace bounded ahead of me up the spiralling stairs, humming to herself. Twice, she tried to step off at the wrong floor, and I had to steer her back on track, but we made it to the third floor without any detours.

Aunt Candace was even more fascinated by the Magical Creatures Division. She kept stopping to examine the furry and clawed books, oblivious to my attempts to warn her off touching them.

"What's she doing up here?" Cass called to us from in front of the door to the fourth floor.

Hearing her voice, Aunt Candace lost interest in the bookshelves. "You're my third niece! I wondered where you'd got to."

To both Cass's astonishment and mine, she bounded over and *hugged* Cass. For a second, I thought my cousin was going to punch her in the face, but she looked too startled to react. After a very tense pause, Cass pried her aunt's arms off her and took a firm step back.

"Are you here because you remember something about this?" She gestured to the door behind her with a hand, casting a swift glare at me that told me never to speak of this again. "Or because you want to take over my shift?"

"Not yet," I said, struggling to keep a straight face, "but Lisa and Walter are both cursed, too, and we're running out of time. The only idea we had is to send someone to look for the curse's source who's part of our family, and since she's already cursed…"

"I get it," she said. "Did Estelle ever find that notebook?"

"No—I thought she left it up here." I scanned the surrounding area, but there was no way I was leaving the pair of them unattended while I went to hunt down the notebook. I'd probably come back to find Cass had turned Aunt Candace into a paperback or something.

"Did that Lisa get her hands on it again?" asked Cass.

"No, but we did have to kick her out of the library for selling dodgy spelled clothing to students." My gaze went to the door behind my cousin, which had returned to its sunny yellow colour, but this time, it didn't appear to be open. *Is the notebook in there? Did the corridor—or whatever lives in there—somehow get hold of it?*

If the notebook contained instructions as to how to find the missing corridor, I could see the security spell not wanting it to get out, but we hadn't *found* any instructions in the notebook. Still, I could always ask Aunt Candace to keep an eye out for it while she was exploring.

Aunt Candace peered at the door. "What's in there?"

"We don't know," said Cass. "Want to go in?"

"Absolutely."

Cass pulled the door open to let her through. Hoping we hadn't made a huge mistake, I watched as Aunt Candace bounded over the threshold and upstairs.

"Sure about this?" Cass muttered to me.

"No, but she's already cursed," I murmured back. "It's not like the corridor can curse her twice."

"Famous last words," said Cass. "Well, it's too late for that now. She's already in."

"I know." I watched her climb the stairs for the moment, her cheery humming echoing in the narrow space. "But if we don't figure this out, Jamie will have reason to pursue legal action against the library and curse all of *us* for good measure."

"Maybe we should invite him to come here and check the corridor out for himself," she said. "Losing his memories can only be an improvement."

"Yeah, but his fiancée got cursed when she wasn't even in here," I reminded her. "Did you hear me say we kicked her out? Well, it's more accurate to say her future husband had to carry her. I knocked her out with a lullaby charm."

She gave a low whistle. "I bet Jamie's declared war on us."

"Pretty much." I heard Aunt Candace's humming in the background as she ambled down the corridor. "Sylvester is watching to make sure he doesn't come back, but there's a limit to what we can do without breaking the law ourselves."

"No kidding." She lifted her head. "What's she doing up there?"

Thumping footsteps overtook her words, and Aunt Candace burst through the door. "I found it!"

"Found what?"

"This." She held up her own notebook. "You were looking for this, weren't you? See, I can be useful."

It was in the corridor after all? "Whereabouts did you find it?"

"Oh, in that strange room with all the mirrors."

"Who put it in there?" None of us had been inside the corridor. At least if it'd been on the stairs, there'd be an admittedly slim chance that a draught had swept it through the door, but not this. Unless the notebook had floated up there of its own accord… which wasn't *that* far out there, but why would it have gone away from its owner?

"Oh, I expect the guardian did." She released the notebook and pen, which promptly began floating next to her.

"The *what?*" Cass and I asked at the same time.

"Who's the guardian?" I reached for the notebook and pen to stop them from drifting away. "Or should I say, *what* is it?"

She blinked. "I don't know. Why did I say that?"

"You tell me," said Cass.

Aunt Candace had already opened the door again. "I'll see if there's anything else in here."

"Wait." I reached for the door, but I didn't quite dare put my foot over the threshold. "Wait. Do you remember going into the corridor the first time? Did the room of mirrors look familiar?"

"A little." Her steps halted on the stairs. "How odd."

"You were cursed up there." I pointed at the stairs. "You're looking for the cure. Remember."

"Right, of course." She continued to climb the stairs. "This place is *fascinating*, isn't it?"

"She's cracked," said Cass. "Even at the best of times, she's unreliable, but this is on another level."

"You don't think it's the corridor messing with her, do you?" I held up the notebook and pen. "This… guardian?"

"Oh, she probably made that up."

"Or her subconscious remembered," I suggested. "We already know something is protecting the corridor by cursing anyone who gets too far in. And last night, I was sure I saw… well, it's weird, but I swear there was someone in there. If not a person, then something that kind of looked like one."

Cass's lips compressed, but she didn't laugh at me. "What did you see?"

"A shadow… it looked a bit like a book-wraith, thinking

about it," I said. "Since it was dark at the time, I didn't see it clearly, but something kept opening and closing the door. And it opened the manticore's cage too."

She made a sceptical noise. "Are you sure it wasn't one of the mobile books? That's far more likely."

"Possibly, but what about Aunt Candace's notebook?" I flipped it open to reveal a page of indecipherable handwriting. "Why would it float up there by itself? It doesn't have a mind of its own, does it?"

"Knowing Aunt Candace, it might," she said.

"Is that more likely than a guardian wandering around and erasing the memories of anyone who goes in there?"

"We know there's something guarding the place," Cass said. "I'm just sceptical of the part about it wandering around. Curses can't do that."

"You'd think not, but…" I trailed off, hearing a loud exclamation from behind the door. "Are you okay, Aunt Candace?"

"Yes, this is spectacular," she called back. "Superb. Thank you for showing me this place, Rory."

"Do you remember anything else?" I asked her.

"No, but I like it in here."

"Great." Cass snorted. "Good luck explaining to my mum why her sister's refusing to come out of the cursed corridor."

"She'll get bored eventually when she can't open the doors." I'd forgotten to get the keys before we came up here, but we'd never confirmed if any of them would work even for a family member. "I hope. I mean, for all we know, that guardian *can* curse people twice. I wonder if we can lure it out."

One would have thought Cass, our resident expert on recapturing magical monsters, would jump on board with the idea, but she shook her head. "A curse has to be cast by a witch or wizard, Rory."

"I know." Ghosts couldn't use magic, either, which invalidated my other theory that my grandmother had somehow stuck around after her death. Unless… "Maybe the Forbidden Room can offer more insight if I ask a less provocative question this time."

"No such thing," she said. "If Sylvester is still in a mood about the corridor getting the better of him, and he will be, we don't have a chance of convincing him to cooperate."

That was what I'd been afraid of, but I couldn't think of any other options. "I can get the keys anyway. See if Aunt Candace can open the doors."

I didn't know if it was the best idea, but I wanted to run the "guardian" theory past my Aunt Adelaide and see if it brought up any new ideas. I was also slightly concerned Edwin was downstairs too… or worse, Jamie.

Luckily, the only people I found in the lobby were Aunt Adelaide and Estelle, who were chatting by the front desk.

"Where's your aunt?" asked Aunt Adelaide. "She's not still in the corridor, is she?"

"Yes—and she found this." I held up the notebook. "It was in the room of mirrors."

"How'd it get in there?" asked Estelle.

"That's what I'd like to know," I said. "Either it floated up there by itself—which isn't impossible, I admit—or someone took it."

"Someone… like who?" Estelle frowned in puzzlement. "Not one of us?"

"Aunt Candace mentioned a 'guardian,'" I said. "I wondered if she was subconsciously recalling what she saw in the corridor the first time. We know Grandma protected the corridor somehow…"

"Guardian?" Aunt Adelaide echoed. "Doesn't sound familiar to me."

Damn. It was worth a try. Still, now that I was downstairs, I might as well put all my ideas out in the open. "I know it's supposed to be impossible, but if this guardian is able to move around, it explains how the curse was able to affect Lisa and Walter when they were outside the library."

"Curses can't move around on their own," Aunt Adelaide said. "Unless they're attached to an object, of course, but nothing has left that corridor that we know of."

"Yeah. I know." I might not have been an expert on magic, but I was certain that the corridor's capabilities went outside of our common understanding. "But it fits with our theory that Grandma set up the corridor to react against intruders and anyone who comes close to figuring out its secrets. Even if they wrote it down in a notebook."

"I thought the notebook didn't contain anything useful," said Aunt Adelaide. "Not that I can read my sister's handwriting at the best of times."

"Me neither." I handed the notebook over to her. "We should probably pin it down so it doesn't float off again. It's not impossible that it went back into the corridor of its own accord, but I was trying to figure out if that's more or less likely than…"

"Than an autonomous spell going around cursing people?" Estelle finished. "I don't know. That corridor confounds me."

"Same here, but I figured I might as well give Aunt Candace the keys for the security doors while she's in there."

"I don't know that that's a good idea," Estelle said. "There's nothing to say she *can't* be cursed twice."

"Yes, that's precisely the problem," said Aunt Adelaide. "We don't need any more trouble. I can only assume Edwin's too busy talking to the shifters to come back here."

"About Walter?" I asked. "That reminds me—I sent Xavier to watch him, but he might be able to help Aunt Candace if she gets into trouble on the other side of one of those doors."

"Well… okay." She reached into her pocket and pulled out the bundle of keys, handing them to me.

"I'll message Xavier first." I took the keys in one hand and pulled out my phone with the other. "See if there's any development on Walter's condition."

"Wise idea." Aunt Adelaide carried her sister's notebook and pen towards the living quarters. "I'll put these somewhere secure."

"Yeah, so they don't wander off again." To my surprise, I got a reply from Xavier immediately. "That was fast. He's on his way."

"Guess there's not much entertainment in watching a werewolf who's forgotten he's human," Estelle remarked. "I hope Jamie doesn't ambush him on the way."

"Nah, he doesn't know Xavier and I are together," I said. "Besides, you'd think even he'd have more sense than to cross the Reaper."

Within a couple of minutes, the door opened, and Xavier entered the library. "Hey, Rory. What's going on with your aunt?"

"I sent her back to the fourth-floor corridor to see if it jogged her memory," I explained. "I don't think she can get cursed twice, but I figured you should be on hand to get her out of there if she runs into trouble."

"I'll do my best, but she wasn't much of a fan of me the last time we spoke."

"True." I led the way to the stairs. "How's Walter?"

"Communicating in growls, mostly," he replied. "Edwin isn't pleased."

My heart sank. "I bet not. We're trying to figure this out, but since the only person who can go in the corridor without being affected is already cursed—oh, we did find her notebook again."

"I didn't know you lost it a second time."

"Yeah, it was in the corridor." I told him the day's events as we climbed upstairs to the first floor then the second. "I have a theory that the corridor is removing anything that it thinks might give away its secrets. Aunt Candace mentioned some kind of 'guardian,' but I don't know where she got that from. Neither does she."

"Guardian?" he said. "You said the corridor was probably equipped with a defensive spell."

"Yeah, but one that can move around." I knew how absurd it sounded when I voiced the words aloud, yet something compelled me to continue. "Everyone says it's impossible, but so is that entire corridor. I could try asking Sylvester, but I only get one question a day, and he didn't take my last one particularly well."

"No… maybe the curse-breaker knows?" he suggested. "Edwin tried to ask him for help with Walter, but Mr Bennet argued that he doesn't deal with shifter-related problems."

"Not even ones that are the result of a curse?" I raised a brow. "I guess he can't remove the curse without access to the source anyway. He told us that himself."

"He's likely trying to get out of being involved," said Xavier as we reached the third floor. "Which I can understand."

We found Cass in the same spot as before but no signs of Aunt Candace. I reached into my pocket for the keys. "Is she still wandering around in there?"

"I assume so." Cass turned to the closed door. "Hey, Aunt Candace?"

No reply came from upstairs. Xavier glided to the door and pulled it farther open, but when I listened, I didn't hear any humming or singing or even any footsteps.

"Erm, Cass, when was the last time you heard her?"

"I don't know. I wasn't paying attention."

"She didn't go into one of the rooms, did she?" No—only

one door had been open. The room with the mirrors. Otherwise, she hadn't had the keys with her.

"I'll look." Xavier stepped past me and climbed the stairs with a Reaper's swift steps.

I remained behind, hand clenched around the keys until they dug into my palm. "Cass, you didn't wander away from the door, did you?"

"No, I didn't." She looked affronted. "I tuned out her singing, that's all. She's fine."

The door opened, revealing Xavier's return. "She's not there."

My heart swooped downward. "Where is she, then?"

"I can try the other doors." He disappeared once more, but the sinking feeling in my chest told me I already knew what message he'd return with.

Aunt Candace had disappeared.

12

Cass and I looked at each other in growing disbelief —and dread, at least on my part.

"Now the corridor is eating people?" Cass said. When I tensed, she added, "Relax, Rory. I doubt she's gone forever. She'll have set off another security spell and fallen through a trapdoor."

"I didn't see anything." Xavier returned for a second time, his expression perturbed. "How long has she been up there? Have you been watching the door the whole time?"

"Don't trust me, do you?" Cass scowled at him. "I haven't moved an inch."

"I never said you did," said Xavier, "but if she unlocked one of the doors, I thought you might have heard."

"Let's see." Cass moved to the threshold, her mouth setting in a determined line. "It's pretty clear that place only responds to family members."

"Don't go in there." I reached for her arm before she walked into the corridor.

Cass shook me off. "Like you wouldn't do the same given half the chance?"

"That doesn't make it a good idea." I dropped my gaze. "We need to tell your mother before we decide what to do."

She grunted. "She'll overreact and close the library."

"Do you really think we should be keeping it open to the public while all this is going on?" It was only a matter of time before Jamie made another attempt to get back at us, and in a more public manner this time.

"No, but I said that from the start, and nobody listened to me." Cass closed the door behind her. "Fine, tell her, and we'll draw straws on who gets to go in there first."

I looked to Xavier, who grimaced. "Ah, I should get back to my boss. I've been avoiding telling him about the corridor, but he'll not be pleased if he figures out that I've been risking myself like this."

"He knows you can't get cursed, doesn't he?" Though who knew; maybe there were some things even Reapers weren't immune to. "All right. I'll tell Aunt Adelaide—Cass, you won't go in there while I'm gone, will you?"

"No, I won't." She planted her feet on the carpet, back to the door, arms folded across her chest. "Go on."

Crossing my fingers that Cass had the sense to stay out of the corridor while we were gone, I went downstairs with Xavier. While he left the library, I explained the situation to Estelle and Aunt Adelaide.

"What do you mean, she's gone?" Estelle asked. "Did she open one of the doors?"

"Xavier said they were closed," I said. "I didn't have time to give her the keys before she went in."

"Why would the corridor take her captive?" Estelle shook her head. "This doesn't add up."

"I know." Guilt churned inside me. "This is my fault. I shouldn't have sent her back into the corridor in the first place."

"It isn't your fault," said Aunt Adelaide. "We all agreed to the plan… and we'll have to solve this together."

"One of us has to go in and get her." I drew in a breath. "It should be me, since it was my idea."

"No way," Estelle said. "There's got to be another way. Sylvester might be able to think of one."

"Have you seen him?" I asked. "Is he still watching out for Jamie?"

"The last I saw." She swore under her breath when the door opened, and a pack of students came in, no doubt looking for last-minute resources for their dissertations. "I'll handle this… can you find Sylvester, Rory?"

"Sure." I ducked behind the shelves and found a quiet spot to call for the owl, figuring that he wouldn't want to talk about secret library matters in front of an audience. "Ah —Sylvester?"

The owl swooped downward and landed expectantly on the shelf in front of me. "Well? Need me to eat some more book-wyrms?"

"No, but Aunt Candace is stuck in the upstairs corridor."

"What do you mean, stuck?"

"She's gone missing," I replied. "We sent her up there to have another look around, since she was already cursed, and she… she vanished."

"How inconvenient," said the owl. "Well, I suppose she's out of your hair now."

"Sylvester, we have to get her out of there." Urgency underpinned my tone. "Two other people are cursed, and Aunt Candace is too vulnerable at the moment to be wandering around there alone. Can you have a look for her? The corridor can't do any harm to you."

"How would you know that, precisely?" he huffed. "I don't remember volunteering to risk my neck."

"You can't get cursed. You're—" I broke off as he rustled

his feathers threateningly. "It's a good thing. Look, never mind. I'll ask Jet instead."

That got his attention. "You want to lose your familiar?"

"I don't want to lose my... why would you say that?" I frowned in suspicion. "You think the curse would affect familiars?"

"If it was me who set up the curse, I would have made sure to close that loophole."

A chill ran down my back. "Xavier is fine."

"He's a Reaper," said Sylvester. "So is your fanged friend. That dim-witted crow of yours, though..."

"Don't be mean," I reprimanded him. "You're not a regular familiar—again, that's a compliment. You can't get cursed. The corridor would have no effect on you."

"That doesn't mean you can use me as your guinea pig," said the owl. "Especially without compensation."

"What do you want in exchange?" I asked. "More bookwyrms?"

"We're talking payment, are we?" He lifted his beak expectantly. "I thought you wanted me to stop that ridiculous wizard from cursing you."

"There is that." Even Sylvester, for all his talents, couldn't be in two places at once. "He's not here at the moment, though, and I'm worried about Aunt Candace. Can you just have a quick look around? Please?"

The owl gave an exaggerated sigh. "Fine."

He took off in a sweep of wings, and I followed, climbing the stairs up to the third floor once more. Upstairs, Cass watched Sylvester's approach with her eyebrows raised. "I thought you were watching for Jamie."

"Your cousin *insisted* I come up here." The owl landed on a shelf near the door to the fourth-floor corridor. "She begged me, in fact."

"Sylvester is refusing to volunteer to get Aunt Candace

out of there without payment," I explained to Cass. "Can you think of anything he might take as compensation?"

"Does that surprise you?" she asked. "I don't know. Try balloons again. Or book-wyrms."

"Not enough," said Sylvester.

I racked my mind. What else did the owl like? Aside from attention? He liked being the centre of knowledge, of course, which was why it bothered him that he hadn't been privy to the contents of the fourth floor. "What about getting to see a new part of the library before anyone else? If you go into the corridor, you'll be able to add its contents to your store of knowledge, and the next time one of us has a question, you'll be able to answer."

Sylvester gave me a searching look, as if he was hunting to find the insult in my words. "You're implying I'm deficient?"

"No, I'm saying that none of us knows what's in the corridor," I said. "Would you rather the rest of us learned everything before you?"

"No." The owl swooped off the shelf and flew through the gap in the door.

Cass gave me an almost admiring look. "You didn't give him the keys."

"Can he unlock doors with his beak?" That one would have to wait until later. "Honestly, I don't think Aunt Candace disappeared into any of the rooms. Not ones that require a key, anyway."

The room with the mirrors was already open, which meant there was a chance she'd disappeared in there, but we'd have to wait for Sylvester's return to know for sure.

Cass moved to the balcony overlooking the lower floors. "What's going on down there?"

"What?" I followed her and heard a distinct growling noise arise from the ground floor. "I don't know."

As someone screamed, my gaze instinctively went towards the door to the manticore's room.

"It's not him," said Cass. "Nobody has opened that door."

Oh no. Had Jamie made a move against us while Sylvester wasn't around? The pitch of the growling suggested either a wild animal or a shifter, and if the latter, I had a sinking suspicion I knew who it was.

"Can you wait for Sylvester?" I asked. "I'll have a look."

The noise grew louder as I climbed downstairs, and as I reached the first floor, I spied a large werewolf below. He ran among the shelves near the Reading Corner, snarling at the terrified patrons, while the group of students we'd let in earlier hid behind the shelves or ducked underneath the desks.

I grabbed my wand, descending the final staircase. *It's Walter.* Why had he come back to the library? Had he expected us to undo the curse? I hadn't thought he'd even understood what was happening.

As I reached the foot of the stairs, Estelle shot a freeze-frame spell at the wolf, causing him to stop in his tracks.

"Everyone outside!" Estelle shouted. "Quickly!"

As the students came out from their hiding places, Aunt Adelaide helped to herd them through the front door. I caught up to Estelle next to the frozen form of the werewolf. "Wasn't he supposed to be at home?"

"I thought so too." Estelle anxiously watched everyone leave through the front door. "Where's Sylvester?"

I grimaced. "He's looking for Aunt Candace. I should have guessed something would go sideways while he wasn't watching the door, but Jamie shouldn't have been aware."

"It's not him who brought Walter here."

"What?" I followed Estelle's gaze as the curse-breaker sidled into the library.

When the last of the patrons left, Aunt Adelaide closed the door, leaving us and Mr Bennet alone in the lobby.

"Did *you* bring the shifter here?" she asked of the curse-breaker.

"Yes," he said. "The only way to undo a curse is at the source."

"That doesn't mean you had to let him rampage around the library," said Estelle. "Don't forget Lisa is cursed too."

"Exactly." His expression showed a mixture of guilt, amusement, and defiance. "You should clean up your own messes for once."

"Jamie was threatening us with bodily harm," I told him. "And Lisa was breaking the law by trying to sell illegally spelled clothing the last time she was in the library. We can't break the curse with either of them around—or a rampaging shifter either."

"Not my problem." He shrugged his narrow shoulders and slunk out the door, which closed behind him.

Aunt Adelaide swore. "Jamie must have convinced him to turn against the library. Where's Sylvester, Rory?"

"He's looking for Aunt Candace," I said. "I convinced him to go into the corridor, but I didn't know Mr Bennet was waiting to ambush us by setting Walter loose in the lobby."

"Oh, it wasn't just him," she said darkly. "I can guarantee he didn't come up with this scheme alone."

Jamie. "What are we supposed to do? We can't bring Lisa back here, and that's assuming Jamie would even let us."

"No, but maybe Mr Bennet is right," said Estelle. "Maybe we do need to take Walter and Lisa back into the corridor to remove the curse."

"How?" I asked. "If the curse was intended to prevent anyone from spreading the corridor's secrets, I don't see it lifting when we bring them back inside."

"I can't think of any other options." Aunt Adelaide tensed when someone knocked on the door. "Who's there?"

Nobody answered, but Estelle sucked in a breath, pointing to the window. "Out there."

I moved to the window, where I glimpsed Jamie standing on the doorstep with his back to the library—and facing the crowd of patrons the shifter had chased outside.

"The library is a sham!" he bellowed with the aid of what I could only assume was some kind of loudspeaker spell. "The owners put a curse on my future wife!"

Oh no. "Someone has to go out there and stop him."

I moved towards the door, but Aunt Adelaide caught my arm and shook her head. "I'll handle it."

Guilt squeezed my chest. Jamie had reason enough to be angry at us, but my family didn't deserve to suffer as a result. "He's dangerous. He tried to curse us, remember?"

"He has an audience," said Aunt Adelaide. "I won't let him slander us in front of them."

Heart in my throat, I watched my aunt walk out of the library, while Estelle held the door open, her wand at the ready in case she had to intervene.

Jamie sneered when my aunt approached. "What do you have to say for yourself?"

"Was it you who set a distressed shifter loose in the library?" Aunt Adelaide asked in a carrying voice. "And—is that your fiancée?"

I followed her gaze and spied Lisa lying on the steps. He must have carried her here, still unconscious, without her being aware. *What's he playing at?*

"What have *I* done?" His voice boomed out, louder than my aunt's. "Your library cursed her. You can't deny it."

"She trespassed somewhere she wasn't supposed to," said Aunt Adelaide. "The library has rules for a reason."

"Nonsense." Sparks flew from his wand as he raised it to point at her. The crowd murmured among themselves, some of them backing out of range, but nobody tried to stop him.

Alarmed, I opened the door farther to let my aunt back into the library. "Aunt Adelaide—get away from him. He's not in his right mind."

My aunt didn't move, not even when Jamie pointed his wand directly at her. "Let's see if we can get some truth out of you."

Acting on instinct, I grabbed my aunt's shoulders and pulled her into the library. The spell struck the door instead, resulting in a shower of sparks. One hit me in the side of the face with a sharp pain like a wasp's sting.

"Ow." I released Aunt Adelaide and stumbled back into the library, touching a hand to my cheek.

"Rory!" Estelle sprang back from the door. "Are you all right?"

"I don't know." My tongue felt fuzzy in my mouth. "I think his spell hit me."

"Don't move." She went to help her mother, who was attempting to keep Jamie from getting inside. *Dammit. I shouldn't have sent Sylvester upstairs.*

Jamie gave me a smirk over her shoulder. "Feel like speaking the truth now, do you? Where is my fiancée?"

My mouth opened of its own accord. "The fourth-floor corridor is cursed to remove the memories of anyone who sees it."

"Say that again?" He grunted when Aunt Adelaide pushed him away from the door with what looked like a herculean effort.

Once again, my mouth opened, the words spilling out. "The fourth-floor corridor is cursed to remove the memories of anyone who sees it."

To my own horror, my voice boomed out, loudly enough for the entire crowd to hear. Had he used an amplifying spell on the whole area?

"That is enough!" Aunt Adelaide shouted, her own voice echoing around the square. "You think putting a curse on my niece is going to do anything but harm you? You *and* your fiancée are now banned from the library for life."

"What is going on?" Edwin's quieter voice nevertheless rang out clearly, and the crowd parted to let him and his troll guards through. "Jamie, I thought I made it quite clear that you aren't allowed to threaten the public."

"I didn't threaten anyone." He stopped grappling with the library door and sullenly watched the elf policeman's approach. "I only convinced that witch to be a little more truthful. Isn't that right?"

"Yes," I spoke, even as a voice in my head screamed at me to stop. "He wanted everyone to know the fourth-floor corridor is cursed to—"

Aunt Adelaide took my elbow—gently—and pulled me out of sight, a finger to her lips. I shook my head, indicating that I *couldn't* stop talking, but Edwin and the troll guards continued their approach. Even Jamie had to move aside when the two giant, grey-skinned trolls climbed the steps in front of the library.

"I'm hearing stories about a rampaging shifter in here." Edwin entered the lobby, his troll guards blocking our view of the square. "What is going on?"

"Mr Bennet brought Jamie here," Estelle told him. "He wanted to cause a public scene."

"His fiancée *was* cursed on your property, wasn't she?" Edwin queried.

"It's her own fault," I said before I could stop myself. "She went into the fourth-floor corridor and got cursed for it, and he decided to cause a scene when Aunt Candace is missing—"

"Missing?" he echoed, while I slammed a palm over my mouth in an effort to stop myself from speaking. "Now you're losing your own family members? *Why* exactly did you keep the library open?"

"The corridor is no threat to anyone unless they go inside," Estelle said. "Which Lisa did—and so did Walter."

"And Aunt Candace," I said around my hand, wishing I could staple my mouth shut. "I sent Sylvester to find her, but I think Jamie must have been waiting for our security to lift so he could make a move."

Edwin's gaze fell on the frozen form of Walter the werewolf. "This is how you dealt with the problem?"

"He was a danger to the public," Aunt Adelaide told him. "Perhaps Mr Bennet is right in that the cure for the curse is inside the corridor itself, but I'm ill inclined to help Jamie now that he's cast an illegal curse on my niece."

"A truth-telling curse, is it?" He gave me a considering look. "That one isn't illegal… and who knows, maybe a bit of honesty would do your family some good."

My eyes burned. "How can you say that? Lisa has a grudge against my aunt, and her fiancé is willing to make a public spectacle of her to prove a point."

"This isn't the first time your library has been at the crux of a spell that affected more than your family," he said. "I'm sorry, Rory, but I've given you the benefit of the doubt too many times. Jamie might be aggressive in his approach, but he's in the right."

"His public temper tantrum doesn't exactly paint him in a good light either, does it?" Estelle said. "His fiancée stole Aunt Candace's property too."

"I've heard enough excuses." He took in a deep breath. "I will encourage Jamie to return home, but I must ask you to apply yourselves to solving this dilemma. I trust you'll manage to come up with a solution."

He left the library, and when his troll guards departed behind him, I caught sight of Jamie outside, smirking at us. Turning my back, I walked past the others, up the spiralling stairs, and scarcely stopped to breathe until I reached the third floor.

"What's up with you?" Cass eyed me in surprise.

I wiped my eyes with the back of my hand. "Jamie cursed me with some kind of truth-telling charm, and Edwin took his side and blamed us for everything."

Cass's brows shot up. "What did you say? Nothing about the vampires, I hope."

"No—but that's another problem." Evangeline would inflict a far more heinous punishment on me than a mere curse if I shared her secrets with the public. "Jamie doesn't have a clue what he's done."

He'd never take the curse off willingly either. No... the only solution was to go to the source of the other curse—or the guardian. It was past time for us to find out what really lay up those stairs.

I drew in a shaky breath. "Cass, I'll take over from you. You can help the others. Or go back to your animals."

"Really?" she asked. "You aren't going to do anything stupid, are you?"

"Yes." The curse compelled the truth to fall from my lips. "But it's the only option."

"If you say so," she said. "You won't tell the others that I didn't try to stop you, will you?"

"Assuming I don't get lost in no-man's-land?" I managed a small smile. "No. This is on me."

I was in enough trouble already. So was the whole library, and the only solution lay behind this door. I might be wary of Grandma's secrets, but I'd solved one of the library's riddles before when I'd faced down the manifestation curse. I could solve this one too.

I pushed the door open wider and stepped in. Silence greeted me on the other side, wrapping around me like a cloak as I walked up the stairs and into the fourth-floor corridor.

13

I didn't know what I'd expected to see when I entered the corridor, even after hearing the description from the others, but for some reason, it took me by surprise to find the corridor didn't look any different to the upstairs in our family living quarters. A simple corridor with plain walls, doors lined on each side, and no traces of anything weird whatsoever. Nor Aunt Candace either.

"Sylvester?" I called out.

Silence answered. *No way. He can't have vanished, too, can he?*

Heart in my throat, I trod down the corridor past a door that lay slightly ajar. I peered in, and my own reflection greeted me from several angles at once, pale and scared looking. Otherwise, the room was lined with mirrors, matching Laney and Xavier's descriptions. It wasn't anything like my dream, but what had I expected? That had been my own imagination, nothing more.

The skin on the back of my neck prickled, as if I was being watched. Out of the corner of my eye, I glimpsed movement in one of the mirrors.

I spun around, but nobody was there. "Sylvester, that isn't funny."

Rattled, I left the room of mirrors alone and moved to the next door. This one was closed, and it didn't open when I pushed and pulled on the handle. I reached into my pocket for the keys and then faltered. Was it a good idea to unravel the rules of this place without help?

"Sylvester, seriously," I said. "Where are you?"

Cass hadn't mentioned seeing him leave, but no answer was forthcoming. Worry fluttered in my chest as I paced down the corridor. A blank wall lay at the end, with no markings upon it. No sign of the owl.

Drawing in a breath, I pulled out the bundle of keys. All of them were identical, so I figured it shouldn't make a difference which I used. Either it would work or it wouldn't, but there was no point in delaying any further. I had all the time in the world now.

I picked a key at random, sliding it into the first door's lock, but it jammed. "Dammit."

I tugged the key then wrenched it sideways, managing to free it from the door. I pushed and pulled the handle again, but it wouldn't give. A laugh bubbled up in my throat, half despairing. *The keys don't even work for family.*

Had I come in here for no reason at all? At least if I ended up cursed, I'd no longer be in danger of spilling the library's secrets against my will if I could no longer remember what they were. That was small comfort, though. I tried another key then moved to the next door.

This is a waste of time. I shoved the keys back into my pocket as I paced back to the mirror room. I scrutinised the mirrors as if answers would appear alongside my reflection, but none did.

As I slumped to the floor, despair rising like a tide,

someone else entirely appeared behind me in the mirror. "Laney?"

"What're you moping in here for?" She stepped up beside me, eyeing the mirrors. "See, this is proof that those vampire legends are a load of nonsense. We're not supposed to be able to see our reflections."

"Oh, that's a myth." I rubbed my eyes. "It's based on the fact that old mirrors were made out of a material that wasn't as reflective."

She gave a laugh. "Did you learn that before or after you came into the magical world?"

"Honestly, I don't remember." I sniffed. "I guess it doesn't really matter. I feel like a complete fool. I thought the corridor was... was sending me a message or something. Trying to get me to come in and unlock its secrets. But I can't even open the doors with or without the keys."

"This one's open." She gestured to the wall of mirrors. "I wonder if your aunt is somewhere in here?"

I shook my head. "If she is, I haven't seen her—and even Sylvester isn't answering me."

"You haven't been cursed yet either," she added. "So that's a bonus."

"Yeah, because I haven't left—yet." I rose to my feet. "If the curse is really chasing down anyone who leaves the corridor, that's one way to lure it out, but it might backfire in my face. This so-called guardian might kidnap me alongside Aunt Candace.

"That's the word Aunt Candace used, though I'm not sure she actually knew what she was talking about at the time." If the guardian existed, it was listening to every word we said, but Jamie's curse made silence no longer an option for me. "Lisa and Walter were both cursed when they weren't at the library, which suggests the curse is able to move around."

Her brow furrowed. "I thought curses couldn't move around. Isn't that right?"

"It is, which is why nobody believes me." No matter how I tried to shut my mouth, the words kept coming out. "Curses also don't take on the form of weird shadowy ghosts, so I understand why the others are sceptical."

"Who made that rule?" she said. "I freely admit I don't know as much about magic as your family does, but this is a library that defies dimensions with a corridor that even your all-knowing owl can't figure out. Why can't it bend the rules of magic too?"

"Don't let Sylvester hear you say that." I smiled all the same. "I know. And I trust my family too. That's the problem. If Aunt Adelaide says something isn't possible, I'm inclined to believe her."

"She's probably trying to protect all of you," Laney said. "This situation is way out of control already, what with that Jamie going around making accusations and setting werewolves loose in here. I heard the others talking about how Edwin made them shut the library too."

"Until we solve this." I heaved a sigh. "All I've done is make myself into the curse's next victim. Sylvester was supposed to help me figure it out, but he's gone AWOL too."

"He's missing?" She glanced up and down the corridor. "Or did he get bored and leave?"

"Either." I shrugged. "He's not happy with the corridor for keeping secrets from him, but he's also immune to curses. Like you and Xavier, but for different reasons. And that's assuming the guardian isn't trying to figure out a way around that."

"Really?" she asked. "If the guardian wants to curse me, it's welcome to try."

"Or Xavier," I added. "At least I didn't start spilling my deepest secrets in front of the Grim Reaper, I suppose."

"Is there anything he doesn't already know?" she asked. "He's aware that we ticked off the Founders, that your father was involved with the vampires, and that you're in love with his apprentice."

My face heated up at the last one. "Yeah, but I don't need the rest of town to find out. Or Evangeline."

"Does it matter what they think?"

"No, but the Founders…"

"They haven't made a move recently," she said. "Despite Evangeline sending me out to look for their hideouts. I'd say they're running scared."

I wasn't inclined to believe they'd give up that easily, but at that moment, a sudden rustling noise echoed down the corridor. Then Sylvester came swooping over Laney's head, making both of us jump.

"There you are," I said. "Where were you? I thought you went missing like Aunt Candace did."

"You complete dustpan." He landed on top of the open door to the room of mirrors. "What are you doing in here? Your family has quite enough to handle without another of you getting cursed."

"I didn't know you cared." The words spilled out, unbidden. "I'm already cursed. Jamie put a curse on me to speak only the truth, so I came in here to avoid causing any more trouble."

"You came to a cursed corridor to *avoid* trouble?" He hooted. "You are an inexplicable human."

"I thought you were going to find Aunt Candace." I gave him an accusing stare. "Did you find her?"

"No," he replied. "I heard the commotion in the library, and it seemed to me that I was more needed elsewhere."

"You didn't stop Jamie cursing me," I said. "Or Edwin from threatening the library."

He beat his wings, forcing me to back against the wall to

avoid the swinging door hitting me in the face. "You have no gratitude."

"I'm sorry, I can't stop—" I clapped a hand over my own mouth, for all the good it did. "Jamie was trying to curse Aunt Adelaide, so at least she isn't the one shooting her mouth off. Really, I'm better off staying in here."

"You're determined to drown in a sea of self-pity, aren't you?" he said. "Would you rather I employed my talons against that unpleasant wizard and sealed your fate in the process? Or chased off the head of the police?"

"All right, you couldn't have helped." I sat down again. "Lesson learned."

"Entirely the wrong lesson, but it's a start."

"Really." Either he'd come here to give me one of his unhelpful pep talks, or he had another reason for coming back. "You figured something out, didn't you? Are you going to tell me what it is or leave me to work it out on my own?"

"You already did, you pencil sharpener."

"Huh?" I frowned. "What did I figure out? That the curse is the result of this... this guardian? Aunt Adelaide said it wasn't possible for a curse to move around."

"Your aunt spends every day of her life governing a library that defies all sense of impossibility," he said. "She does what she must."

I thought back. "If this guardian is responsible for the curse, how do I communicate with it?"

"I would have thought that would be obvious," he said. "There's only one door open in here."

I turned to the mirror-filled room. "Yeah, but there's nothing there..."

Or was there? I hadn't gone *inside* the room or touched any of the mirrors yet. Maybe subconsciously I was still holding back, afraid of what might await on the other side. Afraid I might get trapped too.

Rational though those fears might be, they wouldn't help me find Aunt Candace. Yes, each door, each mirror might hide secret dangers that even Sylvester didn't know about or how to fight against, but wasn't this how my aunts had catalogued the library to begin with? They hadn't always known its secrets. They'd explored each room, one at a time, until they understood.

I could do the same.

I drew in a breath. "I might end up stuck in there, Sylvester. What would you do then?"

"Laugh at you."

"Honestly." Laney shook her head at the owl. "I mean, if you do get stuck, I can get you out. Or Xavier can. Not that I should be encouraging you, but if you're sure…"

"I am." My heart raced, but I stepped up to the nearest mirror before I lost my nerve. "Aunt Candace, can you hear me?"

No reply came, but I reached out and touched the glass with my right palm. "Can *you* hear me, guardian, or whatever you are?"

Was the corridor sentient enough that it knew I was here? If it was like the library in that respect, it must know, but it would be limited in its capacity to communicate with me. Except, perhaps, through the guardian.

"Take me to Aunt Candace," I said to the mirror. "Can you do that?"

The mirror didn't change, nor did it feel anything less than solid beneath my hand. I glanced over my shoulder, but the corridor hadn't changed either. I turned to the next mirror—and a shadowy figure flitted out of sight.

"You!" I spun so fast I nearly fell over, but nobody was behind me but a bewildered Laney. The shadowy figure must be *inside* the mirror somehow. Heart thumping, I faced the mirror again. "You're the guardian, right?"

Nobody answered me, but I glimpsed a similar fleeting shadow in another mirror. *Aunt Candace must be in there too.* Not that I wanted to get stuck alongside her, but I figured there must be a trick to manipulating the mirrors to let me inside.

"Have you parted ways with all your brain cells?" Sylvester yelled from the top of the door. "Or did you leave your magical ability behind with your ability to lie?"

"Magic." I clapped a hand to my forehead. "Right. Thanks, Sylvester."

"What does that mean?" Laney asked. "What—you think your Biblio-Witch magic might help you?"

"We're still in the library, aren't we?" I didn't know if Aunt Candace had tried using the library's magic while in here— she couldn't have, since we'd taken away her Biblio-Witch Inventory for her own safety—but the corridor remained linked to the library. This had to work.

I pulled the Biblio-Witch Inventory out of my pocket, opened it, and tapped the word *find.* Then I pictured my aunt in my mind's eye, and I focused as hard as I could on that image.

The mirror's surface shifted before my eyes, and the shadowy figure appeared at the edge. I exclaimed, reached out my free hand to touch the glass—and my fingertips passed right through it.

I stumbled forward, into the mirror, and my feet touched down on soft carpet. I reeled, finding myself facing a corridor which looked just like the one I'd come in through. Except instead of Laney and Sylvester, Aunt Candace stood behind me.

"Aunt Candace!" I reached for the mirror, but solid glass met my fingers. *Wait—it's a reflection.* I turned on my heel and looked straight into my aunt's baffled eyes. "Hey, Aunt Candace."

"Rory." She blinked at me. "How'd you get in here?"

"Do… do you remember who I am?"

"Yes, of course I do." She scowled. "I managed to negotiate with her to leave me alone. As long as I'm trapped in here, I can hardly spill anyone's secrets."

"She?" I echoed. "The guardian, right?"

"Yes, and now you've gone and got yourself trapped too. Well done."

"I came to get you out." I should have guessed she'd have zero gratitude towards me. "You don't *want* to stay here, do you?"

"I'd have preferred to have my notebook with me so I can make notes, but this place is fascinating enough to make up for the inconvenience," she said. "Did you bring it with you?"

"No, and if you remember everything, you'll know what a nasty piece of work that Lisa Grubbins is," I said. "Her future husband is on a vendetta against the library. We have to get out—"

She cleared her throat and tilted her head. "We have company."

I followed her gaze to the corridor's end, where the stairs were supposed to be. Instead, a blank wall faced us, and in front of it hovered a shadowy form that I hadn't seen clearly the last time. From this angle, it looked almost… human.

"Grandma?" I whispered.

14

The ghostly figure hovered above the floor and didn't react when I spoke.

"She's not your grandmother," said Aunt Candace. "If she was, she would have recognised her own daughter."

True... but her shadowy form was unnerving all the same. "How can it—she—curse people? She's not... not a ghost?"

"No, but she *is* sentient," she said. "Her purpose is to stop anyone from telling tales by erasing all memories of this corridor. My mother was thorough, I'll give her that."

"But you forgot more than Lisa did..." I trailed off. "Because the corridor was a bigger part of your life than for Lisa. You've always lived here."

"You got all the way here without figuring that out?" she said. "You disappoint me, Rory."

"I did figure it out, but what about Walter? He's forgotten he's even human."

Aunt Candace cackled. "Pity that method only works on shifters and not witches like Lisa."

"And you," I reminded her. "What *is* the guardian? It—she—can't be a living curse, surely."

"You've been in the library for long enough to know it's unwise to impose limitations on these things, Rory."

The library. It was sentient, undeniably, but as a result of…

"She's from a manifestation curse," I said. "Like the library itself."

The library was capable of feats that even my family didn't fully understand. It made sense that the guardian would be the same.

"Precisely." Aunt Candace grinned. "A little excessive if you ask me, but who am I to judge?"

"Excessive? She erased your memories." I shook my head at her. "You even forgot you were a writer."

"Yes, well, there are sacrifices that have to be made."

"For what purpose?" As some of my shock subsided, questions bubbled up in my head. "You *were* looking for the corridor, weren't you? You didn't find it by accident?"

"Unfortunately, I didn't count on someone else deciding to come back to town and mess up my plans."

"Lisa," I said. "How much did *she* know? The corridor only erased her memories up to a certain point. She thought she was still at school."

"That's where her obsession with me started."

"Obsession?" I echoed. "She knew about the corridor?"

She lifted her chin. "Not as much as I did, but when we were students at the university, the subject came up. She used to mock me, you know, and when she found out about the missing corridor, she refused to believe it existed. I set out to prove otherwise."

I raised a brow at her. "But it's taken you this long to actually find it?"

"Oh, we both lost interest after a short time," she said.

"Evidently, she didn't forget, and thanks to the impeccable timing of her return to Ivory Beach, she got herself cursed too."

"She got into the corridor?" I asked.

"Not very far." She bared her teeth in a wide smile. "I persuaded her to turn back."

No wonder Lisa had been so irritable when Estelle and I had paid her a visit. "But the guardian didn't get to her until later. What's it actually guarding?"

"Haven't a clue," she said cheerily. "But it's exciting, isn't it?"

"Not if we're stuck here forever." I looked up and down the corridor, but none of the doors from the other side had followed us. Neither had the mirrors. "There's no access to the rest of the library. We'd end up starving to death."

"If one of us has to kill the other to ensure the other's survival, I'm afraid you'll have to make the sacrifice, Rory."

"No thanks." Typical of Aunt Candace to have no regard for the scale of the trouble we'd landed in. My attention went back to the guardian's shadowy form. "Can she understand us?"

The shadowy figure didn't move when I walked towards it, looking at the spot where its eyes would have been. "Can you hear me?"

The ghost said nothing.

"I know you cursed everyone who saw this corridor not to tell anyone," I added. "Even my aunt—your daughter—and me, your granddaughter. You're supposed to make an exception for family, aren't you?"

"She's not going to reply, Rory," said Aunt Candace. "She doesn't have that capability."

"She has enough capabilities to chase down two people at their home addresses and curse them." Most of the library's magic stayed within its boundaries, which suggested

Grandma had pulled out all the stops when she'd designed this place.

When no reply was forthcoming, I turned my back on the ghost and paced down the blank-walled corridor. This must be some kind of prison for people who trespassed and that the guardian couldn't frighten away. Kind of like the Forbidden Room—

Wait.

I was still holding my Biblio-Witch Inventory, and I had a collection of words at my fingertips. One of them ought to work.

I opened the book, and my attention snagged on the word *find.* Before I lost my nerve, I pressed my fingertips to the word, picturing the mirror in my mind's eye.

Nothing happened.

I moved to the next word—*travel*—and focused on the library.

"What are you doing?" Aunt Candace hissed. "You'll get us both killed."

My head jerked up. The shadowy figure had moved closer to us and seemed larger too. The guardian looked down, a pillar of darkness shadowing the pair of us.

I sucked in a breath. "One corridor can't be stronger than the rest of the library."

"Do *not* challenge the guardian, Rory." She backed away as the figure continued to advance down the corridor.

I backed away too, continuing to run my finger down the list of words. *Fly* would have been an option if there hadn't been a ceiling in the way, while *stop* had no effect on a ghost. Neither did *freeze.*

"Have you run out of words yet?" Aunt Candace asked out of the corner of her mouth as we continued to retreat.

"No—*unlock!*" I tapped the page, but with no visible door

to unlock, it had no effect. "The only one left is *summon*. What can I summon in here to get us out?"

My magic wasn't totally powerless in here, I was sure. The corridor was still linked to the library, and while bringing the others in here wouldn't help any of us get out, there was another option.

I touched my fingertip to the word *summon,* pictured the Book of Questions, and squeezed my eyes shut.

A thump sounded, and Aunt Candace yelped loudly. "Ow!"

My eyes opened as she held up the Book of Questions. "It worked?"

Aunt Candace turned the book over in her hands. "What did you plan to do with this, exactly?"

"Use it to get out of here." I reached for the book, conscious of the shadowy figure gliding across the floor. "The book is a shortcut back into the library. I wish to enter the Forbidden Room!"

The book flew open, its pages expanding to fill my field of vision—and blanking out the corridor, including the shadowy figure. Triumph and relief rushed through me, and I grabbed Aunt Candace by the arm as I fell headfirst into the whiteness.

My back slammed down on the floor of the Forbidden Room, and I grinned at the blank ceiling. "Thanks, Sylvester."

"You idiotic desk lamp," he said. "Now you've done it."

"Done what?" I climbed to my feet and saw Aunt Candace had pressed herself against the back wall. "We're out of that corridor, aren't we?"

"Not just us."

Her gaze was fixed on a point behind me, and when I turned that way, I saw the shadowy figure of the guardian in the corner. The figure had stopped its approach, as if being tipped into the room had disoriented it as much as it had us, but it wouldn't last.

"Help—Sylvester, let us out!" I backed against the wall next to my aunt. *Why didn't I realise it would be able to follow us?*

"You aren't leaving me alone in here with it!" Sylvester's voice yelped. "I refuse."

"It can't curse you," I told him. "You're an owl. A room. Whichever. Just let us out."

"I'm not having it wandering around my domain," he said. "I won't allow it."

"Can't you release it into the corridor?"

The owl didn't answer. Maybe he couldn't, since the corridor lay outside of his domain. If he released the guardian into the library itself, she'd be able to curse us again. *We need to stop her.*

"Guardian." I addressed the shadowy figure. "How do we prove we aren't going to share your secrets outside the library?"

"You're wasting your time," the owl said. "She won't listen."

"What if we promise not to tell anyone what's in the corridor?" I asked. "What if we kept quiet? You can't have wanted to keep it hidden indefinitely."

"Yes, she did," said Aunt Candace.

"But she must have known someone in the family would find it," I argued. "Especially if she left the library to us in her will."

"That's it." Aunt Candace's face split in a grin. "Sometimes you have a stroke of genius, Rory. If we find the original copy of my mother's will, it might do the trick."

"But that involves getting out of here," I added. "Sylvester?"

"I'm not talking to you," said the owl.

"Sylvester, if you let us out of this room, the guardian will follow. You know that."

Silence answered. Then the floor of the room opened like a cardboard box, and all of us—Aunt Candace, me, and the guardian—toppled out into the library.

Estelle and Aunt Adelaide both exclaimed as our backs hit the floor beside the desk. "What—?"

"No time to chat." Aunt Candace bounded to her feet. "We need our mother's will."

"What—why?" Aunt Adelaide gawped at her sister. "How did you get out?"

"With this." I picked up the Book of Questions from where it'd fallen to the floor beside me. "But the guardian is chasing us, and she'll erase our memories again unless we can prove we own the library. Where's Grandma's will?"

"I'll get it." Recovering, Aunt Adelaide ran towards the living quarters, while I looked for the guardian and spied her shadowy form hovering near the desk.

"There really is a ghost," Estelle said in a hushed voice. "Is it... Grandma?"

"Not exactly," I said. "She used a manifestation curse and created a guardian for the corridor to erase the memories of anyone who tries to learn its secrets."

"Rory, you can distract the guardian while I get my notebook, can't you?" said Aunt Candace. "Where'd you put it?"

"In a room with your Biblio-Witch Inventory. You'll have to ask your sister which one." I kept one eye on the hovering figure as I moved around the desk. "She put it in there after the guardian tried to steal it back."

"You stole my notebook?" She addressed the ghostly figure indignantly. "That's low."

"There wasn't anything in there on the corridor, was there?" asked Estelle. "Not that I saw."

"You clearly didn't look very hard," said Aunt Candace. "Right, I'll get it."

"No, you won't." I blocked her way to the shelves beyond the desk. "You'll get cursed again, and I doubt Sylvester will be willing to rescue you twice."

"I suppose not." She skirted the desk and followed her sister's path to the living quarters. "Then I'll lie low upstairs until this is over."

"You can't leave me as bait." I watched, alarmed, as the shadowy figure began to glide towards me. Quickly. "Aunt Candace!"

Estelle shouted a warning, and someone tackled me from the side, carrying me into the air—*fast*. I was too startled to do more than yelp as I flew back, and my knees buckled when my feet hit the ground.

"Laney." I looked up dizzily into her face. "What are you doing down here?"

"Rescuing you from a ghost, apparently." She released me, and I belatedly realised she'd carried me all the way to the Reading Corner. "Was that the guardian?"

"Yeah—and she was trying to erase my memories of the corridor." I rubbed my shoulder where she'd tackled me. "Aunt Adelaide went to get proof that we own the library so we can show it to the guardian."

"It's that simple?"

"Give that here!" Aunt Candace's voice rang through the air, and I moved out of the Reading Corner so that I could properly see her and Aunt Adelaide near the front of the library. "Hand it over. I'm the one who's cursed."

"There's no need for that, Candace," said Aunt Adelaide. "Fine, go ahead."

I strode towards the front desk, while Aunt Candace approached the shadowy figure with a piece of paper held aloft.

"This is proof we own the library and the corridor, written in your master's hand," she told the guardian. "Take a look for yourself."

I held my breath as the ghostly figure glided closer to my aunt. Estelle and Aunt Adelaide closed in on either side of her—and even Cass was there too. She must have followed Laney downstairs.

Estelle beckoned to me, and I went to join the rest of my family. We stood in solidarity, facing the guardian.

"The library is ours," Aunt Adelaide told the figure. "You won't harm any of us. We will keep your secrets."

The figure's attention slid between us, paused, and I had the sudden certainty that she was looking directly at me. My heart jumped in my chest. "I'm part of the family. I know we never met, but—"

"Stop babbling." Aunt Candace waved the paper at the guardian. "This says our family owns all of the library, including that corridor. Every one of us."

The figure's attention left me, and the guardian glided across the lobby, disappearing out of sight upstairs.

"It worked." I released a shaky breath. "We're not cursed."

"What about the others?" Estelle asked. "Walter and Lisa?"

"Oh, who cares about them?" said Aunt Candace.

"Their families do," I reminded her. "Lisa's fiancé in particular. And—wait. They don't own the library. How can we convince the guardian to remove the curse?"

"We can't," said Aunt Adelaide. "Which means we're still under threat."

15

Aunt Candace moved towards the stacks. "I'm going to fetch my notebook and Biblio-Witch Inventory."

"Go ahead." I faced Aunt Adelaide, worry seeping through my relief. "What are we supposed to do with Walter? And Lisa?"

"Walter is still here in the library," said Estelle. "In werewolf form, under a stasis spell. Maybe we can bring him upstairs… but that doesn't mean the guardian will agree to remove the curse from him."

"Can we get her to… I don't know, modify the curse so it only covers their memories of the corridor itself?" I asked. "It doesn't make sense for it to erase *all* Lisa's recent memories —or trap Walter in the form of a wolf either."

"It doesn't have to make sense," Aunt Candace said over her shoulder. "They looked where they shouldn't have, and they'll pay the price."

"Aunt Candace." Honestly. Now that she'd been freed from the curse herself, she'd seemingly absolved herself of all responsibility. "We have to stop Jamie from punishing the rest of us and getting us shut down, which means undoing the curse."

"If you want to volunteer to bring Lisa here, keep me out of it." She vanished behind the shelves.

"That's not the plan," I called after her. "You missed the part where he cast a loudspeaker spell on himself and was on our doorstep, yelling about how we're terrible people. He's not going to stop, and don't forget he cursed *me* too."

In truth, I'd almost forgotten myself, but I'd never needed to lie to my family.

"You don't think he'll agree to undo the curse on you if we reverse the one on his fiancée?" Estelle asked hesitantly. "It might be worth making a deal."

"Only if we figure out how to convince the guardian to undo the curse in the first place." I watched the shelves until Aunt Candace returned, triumphant, with her Biblio-Witch Inventory in hand and her notebook and pen hovering behind her.

"Don't look so miserable," she told us.

"Aunt Candace," I said. "We have to fix this, and you're the only one of us who's actually been cursed by the guardian yourself. Can't you help us think of a way?"

She sighed. "I don't know what you want me to say. Lisa is a meddler and a trickster, and she deserved to be cursed. Not just according to me but the guardian too."

Behind her, the notebook and pen bobbed in the air as if in agreement.

"She stole your notebook." I indicated the floating book. "Was she trying to find out about the corridor? Or was she just trying to mess with you?"

"Both." She sidestepped me and saw the shifter, who remained locked in a freeze-frame spell near the Reading Corner. "Have you kept him here the whole time?"

"Jamie and Mr Bennet set him loose in the library to force

us to figure out how to undo the curse," I said. "They're threatening to shut the library, Aunt Candace. We can't walk away from this."

"Deal with him first." She indicated the shifter, while I glanced up at the balcony of the third floor, wondering where the guardian had disappeared to. Back to the corridor, I assumed.

"Why would she erase all his memories, anyway?" I asked. "I mean, he didn't see much of the corridor except for the room of mirrors. That's no reason to leave him indefinitely stuck as a wolf."

"Like I said, the guardian is incapable of distinguishing between someone who trespassed by accident and someone who's a threat to the library," said Aunt Candace. "Now she answers to us, though. Guardian?"

"Hang on a moment." I tensed, seeing movement stirring at the third-floor balcony above. Within seconds, the guardian glided into view at the top of the stairs, as if she'd been waiting to be called.

"That's more like it." Aunt Candace bared her teeth in a grin as the figure glided downstairs. "The guardian knows *we're* her masters now."

"That doesn't mean she'll relinquish her initial goal: protecting the corridor." Nevertheless, I watched the guardian's descent to the ground floor and considered what might convince her to help us. When she reached our family, I asked, "Guardian, can you turn this guy back into a human? I'm sure he won't mind if you erase his memories of the corridor."

"That's true," Estelle said in an undertone. "He didn't see much of it, did he?"

"No," said Aunt Candace. "My own memories were erased significantly, but that's because I've known about the corridor for a long time."

The guardian swivelled towards the shifter… then unmistakably shook her head.

"You won't help him?" My heart sank. "He won't tell anyone what he saw up there, but if we can't turn him into a human again, the library will have to shut down."

"Can it understand you?" asked Aunt Adelaide. "Surely not."

"She understood why we're the masters of the library." I walked up to the shifter's frozen form. "The curse can't have erased *all* his memories of being human, can it?"

"No." Estelle reached for her wand. "I wonder… I wonder if I can try turning him back myself."

"Didn't anyone already think of that?" Aunt Candace snorted. "Honestly."

"We were preoccupied with you being missing and Jamie on the doorstep shouting about us." I nodded to my cousin. "Go ahead, Estelle."

Estelle pulled out her wand and pointed it at Walter, and the werewolf yelped as the spell freezing him abated. He snarled in rage, but Estelle jabbed her wand again, and an instant later, he turned human, crumpling into a heap on the floor.

The werewolf groaned. "Where am I?"

"Walter?" Estelle asked. "Are you okay?"

The shifter blinked. "Do I know you?"

At least he remembered how to talk. "Do you know who *you* are?"

"What kind of question is that?" He looked down, realised he was naked, and yelped, diving behind a pile of cushions. "Why am I here? And where'd my clothes go?"

"You shifted," said Estelle, "and couldn't shift back."

"Weird." He shivered. "Can I have some clothes?"

"Of course." Estelle waved her wand, conjuring up some clothes. "Do you remember who *we* are?"

"No, I don't." He grabbed the clothes. "This is a library, isn't it?"

"Yes, it is." She and Aunt Adelaide began asking more questions, while I spied Aunt Candace trying to sneak off again.

"What?" she said when she saw me looking at her. "I want to check on my notebook. I can't believe that Lisa had the gall to steal it."

"There weren't any notes in there about the corridor." Suspicion arose. "Unless… did she rip out your notes on the corridor and hide them somewhere else?"

If she had, it explained why the curse had hit her so hard.

My aunt stopped in mid-step. "She'd better not have."

"What is it?" Cass asked. "Didn't you get your notebook back?"

"I wondered if Lisa might have stolen the pages of notes about the corridor," I explained. "We didn't find anything in there, and it's where Aunt Candace put all her research."

"That's how Lisa ended up cursed?" Cass said. "Serves her right."

"I don't disagree, but we have to figure out how to stop Jamie from threatening our livelihoods." I followed Aunt Candace as she began a determined march across the lobby. "Where are you going?"

"To pay Lisa a visit, of course."

Aunt Adelaide turned away from the shifter, hearing her sister's retreat. "Where's she off to?"

"We're pretty sure Lisa ripped out the pages of notes on the corridor from her notebook," I explained. "That's why she ended up forgetting the last twentysomething years."

"It's not the only reason, but it's the punishment she deserves," Aunt Candace said over her shoulder. "I'll get those notes back."

"If Jamie is at home, he's not going to give them up

without a fight." I followed, conscious that both Estelle and Aunt Adelaide were occupied with the bamboozled shifter. "Though he does have some of our library books as well…"

"He does." Estelle hurried over to us, eyeing her mother worriedly over her shoulder. "He's dangerous, though."

"Aunt Candace, Jamie has some nasty curses up his sleeve," I warned her. "He cursed me to speak the truth. You don't want him cursing you to give away all your book ideas, do you?"

Aunt Candace merely gave a shrug. "As if anyone else could make use of them."

Then she was gone, the library door swinging shut behind her. I hesitated for an instant before approaching the door myself.

"You're going with her?" Estelle asked. "Rory…"

"I'm already cursed," I reminded her. "He can't do worse… well, he *can*, but I'm the one who set him against us in the first place. Besides, Aunt Candace doesn't know his address, and I do."

"If you're sure," said Estelle. "Be careful, Rory."

Aunt Adelaide nodded her agreement, and I saw Laney watching anxiously in the background. While I could have used all their help, we didn't need to make Jamie even more furious by swarming his house. Best to approach with caution—if Aunt Candace knew the meaning of the word, which was debatable.

Outside, Jamie had vacated the library's doorstep, and the crowd in the square had mostly dispersed too. That wouldn't make them forget what they'd seen, but with Walter back in his human form again, we had one less strike against us.

"Aunt Candace." I descended the steps and caught up to her partway across the square. "I know the address."

"I knew you'd see sense." She grinned at me. "Lead the way, Rory."

I was already having second thoughts—and third and fourth ones—but I'd never get this curse off me unless I faced up to its caster.

While part of me secretly hoped Jamie wasn't in and was scheming with the curse-breaker instead, I knew better than to hope for that eventuality. As we reached his house, Aunt Candace hammered on the door with her fist. "Open up!"

"Can we at least pretend to be subtle?" I winced when the door flew open, and Jamie appeared in the doorway, eyes narrowed in anger.

"You have something of mine," Aunt Candace told him. "Your fiancée stole it from me while I was cursed, and I want it back."

"You want to be cursed again?" He lifted his wand. "I'll be glad to oblige."

"Wait." I tried to catch my aunt's eye and failed. "The curse is on your fiancée because she took some pages from my Aunt Candace's notebook. If you return them, we can..." I couldn't say *we can remove the curse,* because it might not be true, but he got the gist.

"I don't know anything about any notebook," he growled.

"You know I'm telling the truth." He'd seen to it himself, in fact. "The pages contained information that the library wanted to keep to itself."

I closed my mouth, silently willing any thoughts of the corridor to stay put—though admittedly, Jamie being cursed by the guardian too wasn't the worst way this might end.

"There's a simple way to resolve the matter." Aunt Candace raised her wand. "If you don't mind."

Light flashed. As Jamie lifted his own wand, a wad of paper came soaring over his shoulder and straight into Aunt Candace's free hand. With a curse, he fired off a spell that caused a jet of light to narrowly miss both of us.

"Hang on." I ducked as a second jet of light sizzled over my head. "That's all we wanted. You don't have to—"

Aunt Candace interrupted. "And the books too. You don't deserve to get your filthy hands on them."

I grabbed her arm and pulled her out of range of another curse, which hit the garden wall hard enough to knock several bricks out of place. It was then that I spotted none other than Mr Bennet crouching behind the wall, having been forced to duck out of the path of Jamie's curse.

"Get back here," Jamie snarled, taking aim at us again.

I dove behind the wall, as did Aunt Candace, while the curse-breaker shot me a glare.

"What are you doing here?" I whispered. "Having regrets about taking this guy's side?"

"I certainly haven't taken his side," he hissed back. "I have reason to believe this man is hiding illegal cursed objects in his house."

"I wonder what gave you that idea." I dove to the left as another curse struck the wall. I'd have to come out from behind the wall to get a clear enough shot to hit Jamie with a lullaby spell, so I'd run the risk of being hit by another curse.

"He's using one to protect himself, so you won't be able to hit him with anything," said Mr Bennet.

"What?" I lifted my wand to point at Jamie, but my spell veered off to the side. *Oh no.* "It'd be nice if you helped."

"Me?" he said. "I'm a curse-breaker. My role doesn't lend itself to fighting."

"What's the use in that?" Aunt Candace didn't sound nearly as panicked about the situation as she ought to, though she had her wand out too. "Why are you here?"

"I'm calling the police, of course," said Mr Bennet.

"Might be a bit late." Would they get here before Jamie managed to curse one of us? His next spell hit the wall and blew a chunk of brick out of it, leaving a gaping hole.

"You have nowhere to hide now." Jamie climbed through the weed-strewn garden towards where we crouched behind the ruins of the wall.

I reached for my Biblio-Witch Inventory. Its magic was never as strong outside of the library as it was inside, but if my wand didn't work on Jamie, I had no choice but to try my last option.

As Jamie pointed his wand at me, I opened the page and hit the first word I saw—*summon.* If I'd had time to think, I might have pictured Sylvester or perhaps one of the man-eating books to defend us, but as it was, there was only one scary monster at the forefront of my mind.

Jamie's spell misfired as the shadowy form of the guardian unfolded in front of me, and his eyes widened. "What the hell is that?"

"He's threatening the entire library because his fiancée got cursed in your corridor," I told the guardian quickly. "He cursed *me* to give away your secrets."

The guardian might not have understood my words, but she was programmed to protect the corridor she guarded, and right now, Jamie was an unmistakable threat. The guardian advanced on him, and he shrank away, mouth agape.

At least until the guardian drifted right past him and disappeared into the house. *What's she doing?*

Recovering a little, Jamie pointed his wand at me again. "Thought you could send a demon into my house, did you?"

"Demon?" I supposed the guardian did resemble a ghost, but I hadn't the faintest idea why she'd abandoned us. "She's our defender. She belongs to the library."

"Doesn't look like she's doing much defending." He raised his wand, ready to cast a spell—and then another voice spoke from behind him.

"Jamie?" Lisa emerged into the hallway, her hair in

disarray and her strange outfit even more crumpled from being carried around.

He turned, astonishment stark on his face. "Lisa? You remember me?"

Where was the guardian? I turned to Aunt Candace and was met with equal bemusement—then my gaze landed on the curse-breaker. Mr Bennet had turned away, watching the road. There, I saw a pair of trolls lumbering towards the house, Edwin sprinting in their wake.

"What is going on?" the elf demanded between breaths. "Are you destroying this man's property?"

"No—*he* blew up his own wall," I said, glad that the truth-fulness spell worked in my favour in this case. "Lisa took some pages from Aunt Candace's notebook with the details of the hidden corridor, and—"

"And they're harassing me," Jamie interjected. "Trying to break into my property."

"What *is* going on?" Lisa blinked sleepily. "Why are the police here?"

"Because I called them." Mr Bennet stepped into view. "You, Jamie, are wearing an illegally spelled talisman, and I'm willing to bet you have more in your house. Put together with the curses you tried to use on the three of us, it doesn't look good for you."

Jamie went brick red. "You have no proof."

"They also have some of our books," added Aunt Candace, who seemed determined to get the last word in. "I wonder what condition we'll find them in."

"The book-wyrms." My attention snapped back to the house. "Were you behind that too?"

Jamie flushed even more deeply, but Lisa simply blinked in confusion. "Who are you people? Why are you at our house?"

Jamie put a protective arm around her and glared at the police. "You can't prove anything."

"We'll see." Edwin gestured to his troll guards to go forward. "You won't object to us searching your property if you have nothing to hide. Aurora, Candace, go home."

"The books..." I began uncertainly, more worried that they'd find the guardian in there, but then I spotted a shadow drifting behind the ruined wall. *Did the guardian remove the curse? She can't have brought back* all *of Lisa's memories, surely.*

"I'll have them sent to you, don't worry." Edwin waved an impatient hand. "Go back to the library."

"You—" My breath caught. "You aren't shutting us down?"

"No," he said wearily. "I'm not. Though given what I've seen, I doubt anyone *could* successfully shut down your library."

I couldn't help it. I grinned in relief.

16

While I still had a dozen or more questions stacked in my head, the rest of my family deserved answers too. We left Jamie spluttering excuses to the police, trying to deny he'd been cursing us, but Mr Bennet remained to give his own account. The wily old curse-breaker must have been planning to double-cross him from the start.

"Why did Lisa end up getting her memory back?" Estelle asked when I'd finished summarising our clash with Jamie to her and the others. "I mean, she read Aunt Candace's notes, didn't she?"

"Unfortunately," said Aunt Candace, who sat on the front desk, applying a repair spell to her notebook to reattach the pages Lisa had torn out. "Where's that dim-witted shifter? Did you send him home?"

"Yes—and he only lost his recent memories," said Estelle. "He also forgot the library altogether, which seems strange."

"Not that strange," I said. "He doesn't spend a lot of time in here, and when he does, he's usually snacking, you said. He won't miss much."

"There is that." Estelle's gaze drifted up to the balcony, where the third floor was cast in shadow from this angle. "I can't believe you were able to summon the guardian to your side outside the library."

"We weren't that far from the library," I said. "It might have been another story if I hadn't been in Ivory Beach."

"Interesting that the guardian came to your aid." Laney, who'd listened to the whole thing despite her obvious tiredness, kept yawning behind her hand. "Useful too. People like Jamie will think twice about messing with you in the future."

"Yeah, but all the guardian did was adjust the curse on Lisa," I said. "When we left, she didn't know who we were, but she remembered her fiancé."

Estelle's expression cleared. "The guardian must have fine-tuned the curse to remove all memories of the library."

"Her fiancé will remember," said Aunt Adelaide. "He and Lisa planted the book-wyrms, did they, Rory?"

"They must have been in one of the books Lisa returned." Estelle clapped a hand to her forehead. "I should have known."

"Let's hope we've seen the last of them now," I said. "Though Sylvester would be more than happy to eat any stragglers."

The owl himself was conspicuously absent, though I hadn't seen him since he'd evicted the guardian from the Forbidden Room. No doubt he wasn't best pleased about the intrusion, but I hadn't been able to think of a better way to get out of that corridor.

As for the corridor itself... none of us had been up there since our return. Except the guardian, of course.

"I wonder if the guardian will help me catalogue everything in the corridor," said Aunt Candace thoughtfully. "She's our ally now, after all, and now that nonsense with Jamie is out of the way..."

"It isn't," said Cass. "Rory is still cursed, remember?"

My mouth parted in surprise that she'd been the one to remind everyone. "I don't see Jamie offering to reverse it unless Mr Bennet and Edwin manage to convince him. I guess I'll just have to avoid any problem areas until then."

Such as the vampires. After all the work I'd put into hiding my thoughts from Evangeline, I didn't need to expose her secrets for the world to hear.

Laney, who'd otherwise been quiet, caught my eye as if she knew exactly what I was thinking. "Is there really no way for anyone else to remove the curse?"

"No, but it's not the worst souvenir we might have got from this," I said. "I don't mind. I'll just avoid anything to do with the vampires..."

And the Reapers. There were no secrets between Xavier and me, but I didn't need to end up in yet another standoff between them and the vampires.

"Jamie isn't that powerful a wizard," said Estelle. "The library is stronger. It must be able to help, surely."

I glanced at the desk, on which the Book of Questions lay. "I guess I technically haven't used today's question yet."

While I didn't know if Sylvester would have forgiven me for bringing the guardian into his domain, I figured I didn't have much to lose. I picked up the book and flipped it open. "I wish to enter—"

"You're not allowed in." The voice came from overhead as Sylvester himself swooped down to land upon the desk. "I forbid it."

My shoulders slumped, but I put the book down next to him. "Sylvester, I'm still cursed."

"You've already used your question for the day... and for the next few weeks too."

Typical. "Will you accept a feast of book-wyrms in

exchange? Or should I send you to chase Jamie around, pecking at him until he agrees to turn me back?"

"As amusing as that would be, I'm tired." He opened his beak in a yawn. "I thought you wanted to avoid irking Edwin any further."

"True." I glanced at my family members. "Anyone want to volunteer their question?"

"Of course," Estelle offered. "Sylvester, will you show us how to remove the curse on Rory without Jamie having to do it himself?"

"No, I will not."

"Sylvester," I said. "You—"

"I don't have to," said the owl. "She will."

The owl's head rotated to look at someone behind him, and I jumped, seeing the guardian hovering behind the desk. *How long has she been there?*

"I..." I met the ghost's empty eyes. "Can *you* remove the curse?"

"Of course it can," said Cass. "The owl has a point. You're incredibly dense sometimes."

The guardian drifted closer to me, and I held my breath. She might have saved my life, but up close, she reminded me uncomfortably of the Grim Reaper. Maybe Grandma had used him as her model in order to scare anyone out of the corridor.

"Oh," said Estelle. "The curse forces you to speak the truth... which might compromise the corridor's secrets."

"Yes, but I'd rather not lose my memory either." Was the guardian capable of removing a curse cast by someone else? Normally, I'd have said no, but the shadowy figure had already achieved feats that were supposed to be impossible even in the magical world.

Cold air whispered over my skin as the ghostly figure reached out a hand and touched my forehead. My vision went fuzzy, shadows sweeping across my vision as if Xavier had pulled me into the afterworld, and a sudden pressure, which I hadn't even known was there, eased from my throat.

"It's gone." As the guardian released me, I shivered, relieved and spooked in equal measure. "Wow."

My family members wore similarly awed expressions as the guardian drifted away from me

"Better use that request sparingly," Aunt Adelaide murmured when she'd gone. "It doesn't do to play around with unknown magic… but I'm glad it worked."

"No kidding." I touched a hand to my throat. "That was a nasty curse for Jamie to use in the first place. I wonder how Lisa recruited him in her crusade against the library."

"People like him are just looking for an excuse to make trouble," said Estelle. "I hope they both get jailed. Even though Lisa's missing her memories of the library, she still helped him with the book-wyrms."

"I'm going to miss having a nemesis." Aunt Candace held up her newly repaired notebook with a flourish. "Though I suppose I have plenty more on my list."

"Try not to get any of the others cursed, won't you?" Estelle said. "We need to figure out when we're reopening the library."

"Tomorrow," Aunt Adelaide said promptly. "We need to clean up and wait for the police to arrive before then."

———

Edwin showed up after an hour or so with an update—and the books he'd brought from Lisa and Jamie's house.

"They're not cursed, are they?" Estelle asked dubiously as he dropped them onto the desk.

"The curse-breaker thoroughly checked them," said Edwin. "For book-wyrms too."

"Good," said Aunt Adelaide. "We don't need another infestation. I assume Lisa planted them up on the third floor as a distraction."

"Regardless, I do wish you'd told me about the corridor," he said. "Mysterious dangerous doors are a recipe for trouble."

"We'll try to act faster next time," said Aunt Adelaide.

"It would help if the public had a little common sense," Cass interjected. "Also, it's in the library's rules that anyone who enters certain rooms does so at their own risk."

"Yes, well, it does make for tricky legal situations," said the elf. "Jamie is still making the case that his fiancée was cursed on your property."

"She willingly walked through that door," I said. "And stole the notebook. Also, the person who cursed her was technically my grandmother."

I figured the guardian wouldn't mind me sharing that information—Grandma had created the corridor itself, after all. Anyone could come to that conclusion if they knew how our library had originated.

"If Jamie wants to press charges against a ghost, he's welcome to," said Aunt Candace, who was listening in with interest, her notebook and pen hovering at her side. No doubt she'd already set herself the task of finding a way to incorporate recent events into her next book... without ending up cursed again.

Edwin's jaw twitched. "He's not going to. Mostly because he's facing significant charges himself. We found all kinds of illegal cursed objects in his house."

"I knew he was crooked," said Aunt Candace. "He had to be if Lisa wanted to get involved with him."

"This situation is likely to take time to untangle," added Edwin. "I'll let you know if I need you for anything else."

As he left the library, he sidestepped another figure on the doorstep—Xavier.

"Rory." Xavier strode over and drew me into a hug. "I heard Jamie attacked you in public. Are you okay?"

"I'm fine." I beckoned him to the Reading Corner, where I filled him in on everything he'd missed. And there was a lot —from Jamie's curse to my visit to the corridor to our final clash over the stolen notebook pages.

"The guardian removed the curse?" he asked. "All of them?"

"Aunt Candace has her memories back, yes," I said. "And I'm no longer spilling everyone's secrets for the world to hear. Sorry I didn't call you right away. I was worried I'd say something to your boss that would get me blacklisted for life."

"Don't worry about it," he said. "That was a nasty curse Jamie used."

"It seems to be his thing," I said. "The police are raiding his house now."

"Good," he said. "You know, I could have helped you get out of the corridor's trap too. Don't forget I gave you that stone for you to use to call me to your side."

"That would have been my next step," I said, "but Sylvester knows the library, and I didn't want to find out the hard way that the guardian's magic worked on Reapers after all."

"What'll happen to the corridor now?" he asked. "I mean —it's still there, I assume. It hasn't disappeared again."

"We'll have to ensure no more members of the public decide to wander in," I said. "Aunt Candace wants to start cataloguing what's behind all the doors… though she'll have to find a key that works first."

"True," he said. "What was your grandmother hiding in there?"

"Dark and delicious secrets." Aunt Candace walked past with her notebook floating overhead.

"If she is, please don't put them into a book," I said. "You don't want to get cursed again."

"I know the difference between reality and fiction, Rory."

I shook my head as she sauntered out of sight. "Well, it's her risk to take."

"That's right," said Xavier. "Not that it's my business, but it strikes me that your grandmother really didn't want anyone going into that corridor."

"Yeah." The guardian proved that, though part of me remained curious to know what exactly my grandmother had wanted to hide. "The guardian is powerful enough that even our family members need to tread carefully."

"Oh, it should be easy enough to figure out." Cass was next to walk past our spot in the Reading Corner. "I wonder if I can train the guardian to set the manticore loose on anyone who tries to break into the corridor."

"Definitely not." I rose to my feet. "You aren't going up there now?"

"I've neglected my animals for long enough," she said. "But no, I'm not going into the fourth-floor corridor. Yet."

"Good," said Aunt Adelaide. "We need a plan first… and to make sure the door stays in the same place so nobody can wander in there by mistake."

"True." I checked the time. "Want to help, Xavier? We can go on our postponed date afterwards."

"Sounds good to me." He smiled. "It's certainly easier if the corridor doesn't have to be watched twenty-four seven."

"Rory, can you help me with these?" Estelle approached with a stack of books in her arms. "The books Lisa returned. They need to go into the fiction section."

"Right, I forgot about those." The fiction area was right

next to the Reading Corner, so Xavier and I took the stack of books from her to sort out.

"They're all your aunt's pen name books?" he asked. "One from each name?"

"Apparently so." I picked up one of the sci-fi books first. "Lisa's obsession was enduring, I'll give her that. I'm glad she didn't have time to put book-wyrms between the pages… or worse."

Xavier picked up another book and flipped it open. "Is this one supposed to be signed?"

"By my aunt?" I peered over his shoulder and saw the front page had indeed been marked with a thick pen.

Except it hadn't been signed by my aunt.

"Lisa signed it," I murmured. "As if she was going to gift it to someone…"

Then my gaze fell on the name to whom the book was addressed, and my blood iced over.

Mortimer Vale.

ABOUT THE AUTHOR

Elle Adams lives in the middle of England, where she spends most of her time reading an ever-growing mountain of books, planning her next adventure, or writing. Elle's books are humorous mysteries with a paranormal twist, packed with magical mayhem.

She also writes urban and contemporary fantasy novels as Emma L. Adams.

Visit http://www.elleadamsauthor.com/ to find out more about Elle's books.